Gerald began.

"You're touching me now," Veronica said, and opened her eyes.

"I meant . . . you know . . . intimately. . . .
Unless you . . . ?"

The unfinished question quivered between them like an arrow in its target. Somehow it became impossible for either of them to speak or look away. As if a force field had been created around them, currents of energy bounced between their bodies and tugged them toward each other.

A groan—his? hers?—was swallowed in a kiss that went instantly beyond merely friendly. Open-mouthed, hot and needy, this was a first kiss like no other Gerald had ever experienced. Nor was the heat, the need, all his. It poured from Veronica in a response so powerful, it made him shake. Her arms were soft and fragrant bands of steel around his neck, holding him to her as he was holding her to him. Close, but not close enough.

Dear Reader,

Whether it's a vacation fling in some far-off land, or falling for the guy next door, there's something irresistible about summer romance. This month, we have an irresistible lineup for you, ranging from sunny to sizzling.

We continue our FABULOUS FATHERS series with *Accidental Dad* by Anne Peters. Gerald Marsden is not interested in being tied down! But once he finds himself the temporary father of a lonely boy, *and* the temporary husband of his lovely landlady, Gerald wonders if he might not actually enjoy a permanent role as "family man."

Marie Ferrarella, one of your favorite authors, brings us a heroine who's determined to settle down—but not with a man who's always rushing off to another archaeological site! However, when Max's latest find shows up *In Her Own Backyard,* Rikki makes some delightful discoveries of her own. . . .

The popular Phyllis Halldorson returns to Silhouette Romance for a special story about reunited lovers who must learn to trust again, in *More Than You Know.* Kasey Michaels brings her bright and humorous style to a story of love at long distance in the enchanting *Marriage in a Suitcase.*

Rounding out July are two stories that simmer with passion and deception—*The Man Behind the Magic* by Kristina Logan and *Almost Innocent* by Kate Bradley.

In the months to come, look for more titles by your favorite authors—including Diana Palmer, Elizabeth August, Suzanne Carey, Carla Cassidy and many, many more!

Happy reading!

Anne Canadeo
Senior Editor

ACCIDENTAL DAD
Anne Peters

Silhouette
R O M A N C E™
Published by Silhouette Books New York
America's Publisher of Contemporary Romance

SILHOUETTE BOOKS
300 East 42nd St., New York, N.Y. 10017

ACCIDENTAL DAD

Copyright © 1993 by Anne Hansen

ISBN: 0-373-08946-5

First Silhouette Books printing July 1993

Printed in the U.S.A.

ANNE PETERS

makes her home in the Pacific Northwest with her husband and their dog, Adrienne. Family and friends, reading, writing and travel—those are the things she loves most. Not always in that order, not always with equal fervor, but always without exception.

Gerald Marsden On Fatherhood...

Veronica

This fatherhood bit still scares me whenever I think about it—me, Gerald Marsden, a dad. Me, who's never had a family, who's made nothing but mistakes, who's never stopped anywhere long enough to call it home.... Me, a dad.

Fathers are supposed to be wise. They're supposed to set good examples for their kids. But with my past, how in the he—er—*heck* can I be a good role model for anybody, let alone a wonderful kid like Pete?

All I can offer him is love. Is that enough? I've been telling myself it is. I believe that if you love a kid enough, and let him *know* you love him, he'll forgive your other shortcomings. My life's been no shining light for any kid to follow, but maybe the mistakes I made will make me able to guide him away from the bad stuff.

Fathers don't have to be perfect, I keep telling myself. They just have to *be there* for their kids. If not in person, at least with their hearts and souls and minds. I want to be there for Pete. He's been hurt, and I've done a lot of hurting in my time. Now I have a chance to do some good for a change. For him and for me. And maybe that's what this parenting is all about in the end—a two-way street of give and take. The more you give, the more both parties—parents and kids—get back. Such a deal! Given the chance, only a fool would pass it up, and while I may be many things, Veronica, I am no fool. Or at least, not anymore. After all, I married you, didn't I?

Chapter One

Roni's Boardinghouse.

Walking up the cracked and uneven cement walk, Gerald Marsden masked a flash of trepidation with a swaggering walk and what-the-hell expression. He kept his eyes front and center on the house. It looked a lot like some grand old dame gone to pot, he thought, but comfortably so. With its deep, shaded porch, wide bay windows and a front door flanked by ornamental panes of stained and beveled glass, it looked like the kind of house people's grandmas lived in. Respectable. Warm.

Not that he had firsthand knowledge about grandmas, never having known his own. And when it came to respectability... Well, he'd never had more than a nodding acquaintance with that, either.

But that, Gerald reminded himself as he took a deep breath and pressed thumb to doorbell, was neither here nor there.

Clearing his throat, squaring his shoulders, Gerald was about to ring again when the door was opened and he found himself facing an elderly, white-haired and somewhat lumpy woman through some twenty inches of opening.

"Yes?" she said, her tone cautious as she near-sightedly squinted up at him.

"Roni?" asked Gerald.

Her curt, "No," brought home to Gerald that looks were generally deceiving. This little old lady might *look* like everyone's fantasy grandma, but any grandmotherly sweetness was strictly exterior. "You the fella called about the room?"

"Yes, ma'am, I am. Name's Marsden. Gerald Marsden."

"How do." She didn't move, didn't open the door any wider and didn't introduce herself back. She only stared at him, unblinkingly and with lips pursed.

She's no dummy, Gerald thought, shifting his weight from one foot to the other as she studied him. She's gonna take her time and look you over before letting you in, bud. Which was great, except that as the moment stretched into another, he grew uncomfortable.

Propping one hand against the doorjamb, he cleared his throat. Maybe she was waiting for him to say something else. "Er, you the landlady, ma'am?"

"Nope." She backed up a step, assessing him, her stare narrowing. "So what are you?" she asked. "Thirty-five, six? On the phone you never said."

"Well, er—" Though the ad had specified 'Males only; under 40,' it hadn't occurred to Gerald to mention his age. "I guess that's because you didn't ask."

"So I'm asking now."

"Okay." He shrugged. "I'm thirty."

"Hmm." This earned him another, more thorough once-over, and, just for a moment, Gerald wondered if something about him still bore the stamp of—

But no. He was being paranoid. Big Mike had told him to be careful of that kind of thinking. The month he'd spent at Peggy and Bill's in Lauderdale before coming to Oregon had tanned his face and weathered the newness out of his clothes. He didn't look any different from anybody else. So why did the old lady keep eyeballing him like she didn't know whether to let him in or shut him out?

"Look, lady…" he began, thinking did he really need to board in a house with someone as peculiar as this old bird, when she obviously decided it was okay to let him enter.

"So all right," she said, her tone downright cheery all of a sudden. "Come on in. Roni—that's my niece—she isn't here right now, but seein' as how you *are*…" To Gerald's amazement, she giggled as if delighted by something. "No harm in you comin' in."

"Thanks." Stepping inside, the illusion of entering a preadolescent daydream intensified. The house's interior was just as he used to imagine a grandma's house to be—with an old-fashioned bureau type thing along a wall of dark wainscoting and striped wallpaper, and with the rich smell of coffee and something baking in the air.

Looking around, inhaling the tantalizing scents, Gerald's gaze was snagged by the old lady's. He gave her a twisted half smile, and the smile she gave back now had some of the sweetness her tone had earlier lacked.

"I'm Louise Upshot," she said.

"Pleased to meet you."

"You'll have to pardon the ruckus," she went on, nodding toward partially open French doors through which a burst of laughter and lively conversation spilled out into the foyer. She was moving ahead of him up the stairs to the second floor now, wheezing a little from the exertion of the climb.

"Old Miz Henks, she's in the room next to the one you'll be lookin' at. She's seventy-five today and we're doing a bit of celebrating. Been with us ever since we opened, she has. Goin' on eight years now, can you believe it? Anyway, she used to be the librarian here in town. Never could have children, poor dear, and now she's got no family a-tall. You got family, young man?"

"No." The wallpaper in the stairwell had pink roses on it.

"Unattached, are you?"

"Yes." And at the open hall window, starched white curtains billowed in the breeze. Nice, Gerald thought.

Ahead of him, Louise opened a door, stepped aside, and waved him into a large, bright room dominated by a massive, oak four-poster. "All our people are decent, quiet folks," she told him. "Some of them, Miz Henks in particular, are frail, you know. We don't hold with loud carrying-ons here."

"I understand." Gerald carefully sat on the bed to test the mattress. It was firm. He stretched out on it and looked up at the ceiling. No cobwebs there, just gleaming whiteness and a curlicued light fixture of milky glass. The bed felt solid and his feet didn't dangle over the end of it. At six-five, two-thirty, those were important factors he'd never before had the luxury to consider.

"No rough stuff," Louise continued, with a pointed glance at his well-muscled frame, bristly cheeks and longish, not quite tidy hair. He'd been so pleased just to be able to let it grow again, he hadn't given a thought to neatness and style. "And no smoking, mind. Of any kind," she added, "if you know what I mean."

"Yes, ma'am." Knowing very well, Gerald suppressed a grim smile and the temptation to point out that for quite some years now pot was not what she should be worrying about.

"I know how you young folks like your music." Louise opened a window and gestured with her hand for Gerald to come see. "Nice view of the backyard from up here. Rufus!" she hollered at a mangy shepherd in the yard next door. "Quiet!" As the dog instantly subsided into tail-wagging silence, she explained, "He's only out when Marge runs her errands."

Closing the window, seemingly never stopping her monologue for breath, she returned to her original topic. "Lord knows, a few years back Roni could listen to that rock 'n' roll music by the hour." She eyed his hair and face again, as well as his T-shirt and jeans. "I expect you did, too. You got a guitar?"

"No." Humor half lifted one corner of his mouth. Obviously the old lady had him pegged for some kind of latent hippie. "No guitar," he assured her solemnly. "Matter of fact, not even a radio."

That seemed to take her aback. "Oh?"

"No. See, I'm not from here. I'm, er, making a new start here in Salem, so to speak."

"Hmm." Some of the caution was back. "So where're you from?"

"Ah, back East. You know, Maine." Gerald opened and closed dresser drawers to avoid meeting her gaze.

"Maine, huh?" A note of uncertainty quivered in her voice. "That's a fair piece away from Oregon."

"Sure is." Which was exactly why he'd come.

"Lived there all your life, did you?"

"Uh, no." He really didn't want to get into all that, didn't like it when people pried. On the other hand, what could it hurt to admit he'd lived—if you could call it that—in Boston?

He told her, and even went so far as to say, "From about age fourteen. Before that I, uh, lived mostly in Springfield." Under the guise of studying the faded print of a seascape above the dresser, he groped for some bit of small talk that would conclude this subject.

"You ever been to Massachusetts?"

"Nope. Never got farther east'n Denver and that was just fine by me." She paused. Gerald tensed, but relaxed again when he heard her next question.

"You got a job?"

That one he could handle. "I do," he said and, after a cursory inspection of the room's small closet, finally faced her.

"You planning to stay in these parts, then, I take it?"

"Don't see why not."

"You got money?"

He nodded. "Some."

"Room and board here's three hundred dollars, you know. And payable in advance every first of the month."

"So the ad said."

"No exceptions."

Gerald bit back a smile. "I understand."

"Hmm . . ." She preceded him back out into the hall and turned to him once more with her lips pursed so tightly, deep furrows encircled her mouth like a kid's drawing of rays sticking out from a pink crayoned sun.

Obviously, she was giving some very deep thought to the pros and cons of taking him in as a tenant.

Gerald did his best to look nonchalant, but the truth was, gaining this old lady's approval seemed to have become important to him. He really liked the house and the room, and the idea of tramping all over town looking for someplace he knew he wouldn't like nearly so well held no appeal. Which was why he felt as though a load of bricks had dropped off his chest when Louise's prune-mouthed contemplation of him abruptly relaxed into a broad smile.

"Well, son—" Her dentures were fully on display. "Room's yours, if you want it."

"I want it all right."

"Good." Hands clasped in front of her drooping bosom, she gazed up at him, visibly pleased. "So what do they call you? Jerry?"

"Sometimes." From the time he'd reached his full growth, "Moose" was what he'd been called. He didn't want her knowing that, though. It seemed too . . . crass in this new life of his.

"Well, I think maybe Gerald suits you better at that. My—" she patted his arm and let her hand linger "—you're a big'un, aren't you? Solid." She emphasized that observation with a nod and a tightening of her hand on his arm. "I like that in a man. I expect you like to eat, huh?"

"Yes, ma'am."

"Well then, Gerald, you've come to the right place. We serve good, down-home cookin' in this house."

"Sounds great." In fact, it sounded fantastic. Just thinking of it made saliva pool in Gerald's mouth. He hadn't eaten since breakfast eight hours ago.

"Good." Louise was eyeing him with such motherly approval, Gerald felt the queerest tightening sensation in his throat. He was glad when all of a sudden she turned brisk again.

"All right now, pay attention." She pointed. "Lavatory on your left, bathroom one door down. No shower, mind you, just a tub with a hand-held sprayer."

"It'll do."

"You share it with Judge Cunningham. He's a sweetheart . . ."

Judge? Gerald mentally stiffened. He'd met his share of judges over the years and none of them had been 'sweethearts.'

" . . . been retired eleven, no, twelve years now. A circuit judge, you know. Never married, but a nicer man you couldn't hope to meet." She closed the bathroom door. "You'll have to work out a schedule with him."

"No problem." So why shouldn't there be nice judges, too? With some impatience, Gerald silenced the part of him that was recoiling. This was now. *Then* was over.

"There's another bath across the hall that old Miz Henks shares with Leo Kominsky," Louise said, heading back down the stairs with Gerald in tow. "Leo used to be in shoes. Wholesale, don't you know. Traveled all over."

"That so." Seemed like nobody had any secrets in this house. Except him.

"Wife divorced him on account of she didn't like his traveling all the time. His kids're grown now, o' course. One's in Ohio somewheres—a doctor. The other's overseas on some fancy engineering project. What line o' work did you say you were in, dear?"

He hadn't said. "Construction."

"Really?" She stopped to turn and squint up at him. "My George was a master carpenter, you know. From the old country. Built this house mostly all by himself more'n fifty years ago. You a carpenter?"

"No, ma'am." By now, with someone else, Gerald might have gotten real uptight about all those snoopy questions, but he figured the old lady didn't mean any harm, and that she was entitled. "Jack-of-all-trades, you might say."

"Hmm." Louise turned to go down the last couple of steps. "I expect that's how you got all those muscles then, working."

"I guess," Gerald said, not seeing any reason to point out to her that it hadn't been by merely working, but by working *out* that he'd gone from just naturally big to impressively powerful. That years of lifting weights, running laps and punching the stuffing out of punching bags had been what had done it. That that's how he'd finally learned to handle a lifetime of accumulated rage, and that physical exercise had replaced physical violence as a release valve when things would start to get to him.

Downstairs now, they passed the party again. It had apparently settled down some.

"They're eavesdropping, you know," Louise confided with a wink. "Come on—" She pushed one half of the French doors all the way open and beckoned Gerald next to her. "Make 'em happy. Stick your head in and tell 'em hi."

Feeling a bit self-conscious, Gerald reluctantly humored her and saw five curious elderly faces look expectantly back at him from beneath colorful paper party hats.

"Judge," Louise called out to a heavyset man with a cherub's face beneath a halo of grizzled curls. Santa Claus, Gerald thought, and as his eyes met the judge's shrewd ones, added, But nobody's fool.

" . . . Miz Henks, Leo . . . Everybody, this here's Gerald Marsden. I'm gonna let him have the room."

There was a hearty male chorus of "Hello, son," and "Oh, my!" from two girlish voices. The judge, however, took his time responding and kept his gaze squarely on Gerald's. One bushy brow arched in the course of this inspection and his eyes, narrowing, grew shrewder still. He looked thoughtful for a moment, but when Gerald—thinking, He knows. He knows—neither blinked nor looked away, a small smile crooked his mouth and, nodding, he gave Louise a wink and an okay sign which she acknowledged with a pleased nod.

Gerald let go the breath he hadn't noticed he'd held. With his gaze once more connected to that of the older man, he, too, nodded. It was a silent promise—he couldn't have said of what. But even so, somehow he knew that the other man had understood. The knowledge came with a rush of unexpected warmth.

Discomfited by emotion, he stepped away from the door, mumbling, "So those're the boarders, huh? Nice people."

"Salt o' the earth," said Louise proudly. As if in a hurry now, she was hustling him up the hall. "'Course, only three of them live here," she explained. "The other two are friends from the Senior Center. . . ."

She ushered Gerald through another door into what turned out to be a spacious kitchen. The good smells intensified and Gerald saw that the source—a cake—sat on the large, round wooden table in the middle of the room. Judging from the mess of dirty utensils sur-

rounding it, it had only recently been baked and deco-
rated.

Louise pulled out a chair. "Go ahead and sit." She
chuckled gleefully, rubbing her hands. "We're gonna
get you all signed, sealed and delivered before Roni
shows up."

Wondering why this might be important, Gerald took
a seat while Louise rushed to a drawer, snatched up a
dog-eared journal and hurried back with it to the table.
She perched herself on a chair across from him and
stuck a pair of glasses on her nose.

"So that'll be three hundred dollars then."

"Oh, sure." Shifting, Gerald extracted a billfold from
the back pocket of his jeans. "Cash all right? I don't
have a bank yet."

"Cash'll do fine, dear." Louise was already writing.
"When're you planning to move in?"

"Today, if I could."

She shrugged. "Room's free. And you can park your
car in the back alley."

"Thanks but—" After taking out four fifties and five
twenties, Gerald stuffed the wallet back in his pocket.
"—there's no car."

"Oh?" Louise glanced up, surprised. "How'd you
get here, then?"

"I walked from the bus depot. My stuff's in a locker
over there."

"Oh?"

"All I've got is my clothes."

"Oh?" Louise frowned at him. "You been in the
army, son?"

"No."

"College?"

"No." Gerald felt tension and dread begin to roil in his gut like a bad case of indigestion.

"So where you been?"

"I—" Biting his lip, Gerald's hand fisted around the bills in his hand, crushing them. He'd hoped she wouldn't ask like that, point-blank. He'd made a pact with himself—from here on in he'd be straight, especially with people who mattered.

Damn. Gerald closed his eyes against a surge of discouragement, thinking, There went the room. Why the hell hadn't he just let that Frank Tillman guy downtown line up some digs, and forget trying to bury the past?

On a deep breath, he forced himself to look straight into Louise Upshot's faded blue eyes. Behind her spectacles, they were larger than normal eyes were. And kind. Gerald knew they wouldn't be for long, though.

"I—"

"Gerald." Louise reached across the table and laid a warm, wrinkled hand over his fisted one.

Gerald's first impulse was to jerk away, but he made himself relax.

"Are you in some kind of trouble, son?"

He took another deep breath. "No, ma'am, I'm not." Should he just leave it there? It was true, but . . . Come clean, man. Do it. "Thing is, though," he went on, "up until about five weeks ago, I was in a—"

God, but the truth was hard to spit out.

She interrupted. "You didn't leave a wife'n fam'ly stranded somewheres, did you, boy?"

Him, the loner, with a wife and kids? The idea was so ludicrous, it almost made Gerald laugh. He closed his eyes instead and slowly shook his head. "No, ma'am, nothing like that. Truth is—"

"No, dear," Louise interrupted again, decisively. "Don't say no more now, you hear me? I can see it's costin' you to talk about your life, and if there's one thing I learned at my age, it's that a body's entitled to their privacy. You tell me you're clean..."

Gerald nodded, meeting her gaze.

"... and you tell me you're unattached..."

Another nod.

"...and that's good enough for me. You're fine, boy. Jest fine." After giving his hand a motherly pat, she withdrew hers and resumed filling out the receipt. "I say let's get this over with and go have us some birthday cake."

Right at that moment, Gerald would have given anything to be able to tell this old lady how much her generosity of spirit meant to him. But aside from anger, he had never learned how to show the emotions he felt. And while he'd finally learned to express that anger— anger at himself, at the mother he'd never known, at society in general—in ways that weren't harmful to himself and others, he still had a long ways to go, where expressing things like friendship, love and kindness were concerned.

And so, feeling inadequate, he cleared an irritating roughness out of his throat and gruffly extended the cash. "Well, then, here's your three hundred." His throat worked soundlessly for a minute before he was able to add, "And, uh, thanks."

"Bah." Louise waved the word away. "Just don't make me sorry, that's all." Rising, she ripped out the receipt and handed it to him. "There. And you can call me Louise now."

Louise. She was quite a lady.

They exchanged a smile some might have called fond, and Louise was just stuffing Gerald's money, uncounted, into a cookie jar shaped like a pink cat sitting down, when the back door flew open with a bang.

Rump first, a tall, dark-haired woman came into the kitchen from the back porch. As she swung face front, only a pair of darkly lashed, very green eyes beneath straight brows were visible above the two bulging bags of groceries filling her arms.

She remained framed in the doorway for a moment, her gaze tangling briefly with Gerald's at the table.

"Oh," Veronica said, startled. "Hi." It wasn't every day that men who looked like rumpled and unshaven Patrick Swayzes graced her kitchen table.

She was tall for a woman, Gerald noted. Five-ten or more. Her voice was husky like a whiskey drinker's voice, though judging by her prissy dress and ruthlessly pinned-back dark hair Gerald doubted that's how she'd come by it. Still, the sultry sound made something hot and primal flare in his gut and sweat pop out on his forehead. Down, boy. Get a grip!

Brusquely severing eye contact and grimly tamping down the unwelcome flash of heat and awareness, Gerald directed a clipped, "Hello," to the wall beside her head.

Taken aback by the man's curt tone and inexplicable scowl, Veronica's gaze veered toward Louise who was bustling around the table with arms outstretched.

"Welcome home, Roni dear," she was saying, offering her cheek for a kiss as she enfolded her niece in a hug.

"Hi, Aunt Lou."

Veronica bent to kiss her aunt as Louise relieved her of one of the bags, saying, "So how was school today, pussycat?"

"Murder, as usual, thank you." Setting the remaining bag on the counter, Roni's gaze was drawn back to the forbidding stranger at her table and she caught him looking at her. Disconcerted because now he appeared amused rather than angry, she blushed and grew more flustered still. "Thank God I don't have to teach every day," she babbled. "Anyone who says seventh graders are a menace obviously hasn't subbed in a fifth-grade class. But tell me—"

She was disturbed, Gerald thought, amused. By him. Just as he'd been disturbed by her before she'd set down those grocery sacks and he'd seen the rest of her face. Not that it was ugly, that face. No, no, nothing that dramatic. It was only...*plain,* Gerald supposed, was probably as good a word as any to describe it. Plain nose, plain cheeks, plain mouth.

And in all that plainness those disturbing green eyes of hers no longer seemed vivid, and that disturbingly smoky voice was merely pleasant to the ear instead of tantalizing.

Liking things—her—much better this way, he relaxed and prepared to enjoy the interplay between niece and aunt.

"Aunt Lou, what have you been up to?"

"Up to?" Louise busied herself with the groceries, then smiled—a little too brightly, Gerald thought—at her niece. "Why, nothing, darlin'. Except Miz Henks's birthday and, well, Gerald here, o' course."

"Gerald?" Roni asked, her gaze returning to the man with distinct reluctance. Though not classically handsome, he exuded something, an earthiness, a *masculinity*, which at once drew and repelled her.

Adding his unsettling presence to Aunt Lou's all-too ingenuous air of innocence had Roni's antennae shoot up. Something was going on. Something she had a feeling she wasn't going to like. It seemed to her that the last time her aunt had acted as suspicious as this had been the time Louise and the other boarders had invited the Reverend Mr. Petersen for afternoon tea, only to promptly lie down for their naps as soon as he'd showed up, leaving Veronica to feed mint tea and oatmeal cookies to the most boring man on the face of the earth.

Matchmaking...how her old folks *loved* to do it. Just because she'd announced some time ago that marriage was not for her—she truly did like her life just fine the way it was—and just because they disagreed with her on that...

Oh, no. Veronica's gaze, still on the stranger, widened with dismay. Surely, they wouldn't...

But, of course, they would. The headache she'd been fighting all day now exploded into a full-blown migraine. "Aunt Louise..."

"I'm sorry, pussycat—" Louise went to stand beside her visitor and donned a hostessy smile. "—I should've introduced you sooner."

With bewildered wariness, Roni looked from one to the other, from her aunt's beaming visage to the man's wryly apologetic one.

"This here's Gerald Marsden, darlin'," said Aunt Lou in a tone that suggested she was making Roni a very special gift. "Gerald, meet Veronica Sykes, or Roni as we call her." She laughed. "Dear Roni..."

She eyed her niece fondly, making Roni grind her back teeth. "She's my dead brother's only child, don't you know, but George and me, we raised her like our very own daughter from the time she was knee-high to a grasshopper. Which wasn't always easy, but, hey, what's family for if not—"

"Aunt Louise." Even more than the gleam in Louise's eye and the too-fond expression, her aunt's lengthy speech reinforced Roni's conviction that there was mischief afoot. It took considerable effort to find a polite smile to give to Gerald Marsden along with her hand.

"How do you do, Mr., uh..." In her agitation, she faltered, groping for the name.

"Marsden." Both the man and Aunt Louise replied, and Veronica's disquiet grew at her aunt's eagerness.

Gerald rose to shake his landlady's hand and found that the warm, firm slenderness of Roni Sykes's hand in his felt way better than a handshake between indifferent strangers had any business feeling.

His "Glad to know you" was subdued, and it irked him to see that Veronica, who'd yanked her hand from his as if away from a live wire, was now surreptitiously wiping it against the side of her skirt.

"Was there something I can do for you?" she asked him as coolly as she was able, given the jolt she'd gotten from the touch of his hard, callused hand.

"Yes," said Louise in Gerald's place. "A little later, you can drive Gerald here over to the bus depot."

"Oh." He was leaving. Suddenly Roni felt foolish for her suppositions, suspicions and silly reactions. She wasn't this easily thrown off balance as a rule, even by her aunt's and the boarders' occasional shenanigans.

Another flush, this one of chagrin, scorched her cheeks. "Why, sure," she told Gerald, even managing a genuine smile this time. "I'll be glad to take you."

Amazed by what a smile could do to a face, Gerald was too stunned by the transformation in Roni's appearance to smile back, and only stared at her.

Roni tried to look away but couldn't, and unnerved by the flutter of reaction someplace deep in her belly, somewhat breathlessly asked, "So where're you headed?"

"Gerald's not headed anywhere." Aunt Lou again. "He just got into town. From Maine."

"Oh?" No one had ever looked at Roni with such unrelenting intensity. It made her feel like some predator's coveted morsel, which should have been unpleasant, but wasn't.

"His luggage is still at the depot, is what, pussycat. You see, Gerald here's gonna stay for a while."

"Oh?"

Roni's gaze was still trapped by Marsden's, which, incredibly, was beginning to crinkle with humor again when Louise finally got to the point and said, "He's the new boarder, don't you know."

"What!"

Gerald couldn't help it. He laughed. Veronica Sykes's slack jaw, rounded eyes and high-pitched exclamation of shock confirmed his growing suspicion that by renting him that room, good old Louise had somehow pulled a fast one on her niece.

He couldn't quite figure how and why, but, man, that green-eyed lady was upset!

"Aunt Louise." Veronica was seething. This time her aunt had gone too far. "Are you telling me that you . . . that this man . . . ?"

"You bet." Louise was all round-eyed innocence. "He answered the ad, sweetheart."

"The ad? Which ad?" Though striving for calm, Veronica heard her voice shoot up an unflattering octave. "I haven't even placed one yet!"

"Well, ah . . ." For an instant, Louise faltered in the face of her niece's fiery-eyed ire. But then she raised her chin and firmed her tone. "We went ahead and placed one for you."

"We?"

"The others and I."

Bingo! Praying for strength, Roni closed her eyes and deeply inhaled. *The others and I . . .* She'd been right to be suspicious. She'd kill 'em, but first . . .

"Aunt Louise," she said with all the dignity she could muster, under the circumstances. Chin high, avoiding his eyes at all cost, she brushed past Gerald Marsden and headed for the door. "Could I see you in the hall a minute? Please."

Gerald didn't know what had been said out in that hall, but whatever it was, Louise returned to the kitchen with a wink and thumbs-up to invite him into the living room for some coffee and cake.

Roni had been cool to him, but civil. But she'd cut the others cold. Probably with good reason, Gerald had supposed, since every one of the boarders seemed to have trouble looking her in the eye. They were guilty of something besides putting an ad in the paper without her knowledge, he just couldn't figure out what until driving back from the depot to the house, he asked Veronica and she told him.

"Matchmaking."

He gaped at her, dumbfounded. "You mean as in . . . ?"

"Getting married, that's right."

"Married?" he gasped. "You and . . . and *me?*"

"Uh-huh."

That cracked him up. After all, given who and what he was . . .

"That's the most ridiculous thing I've ever heard."

"Humph!" Roni tossed her head, the look she shot him a mixture of pique and contempt. "Likewise, I'm sure."

Chapter Two

No doubt about it, Gerald thought waiting silently for Veronica to hand him his lunch bucket, things between himself and the landlady had not improved since that inauspicious first day a week ago.

'Course, in the car with her, he shouldn't have laughed the way he had. It had hurt her feelings. She thought the idea of *him* marrying *her* was what he'd found so preposterous when really it'd been the other way around.

Not that he'd told her that. And not that he thought this matchmaking stuff made any sense. It didn't. In fact, he didn't blame her for being ticked off with those cantankerous old busybodies. All he'd like to know was, was that any reason to keep on treating him like a leper?

Roni didn't like Gerald Marsden, though she couldn't have said precisely why. All she knew was, ever since he'd come to live in her house, she had been wound tighter than a string around a top, and if ever she let go she'd be spinning just as crazily, too.

The man irked her. He bothered her. And not by anything he said or did so much as by just *being*.

He was so big, so... so *physical*. Whenever he came into a room, he seemed to fill it. Even without his saying a word he somehow captured her attention.

And always gnawing at the back of her mind was the humiliating knowledge that as a woman—as matrimonial material—he found her laughable.

She wanted him gone.

Roni slammed shut the cookbook she'd been leafing through in search of a meal plan for dinner and tossed it aside. Needing something or someone on whom to vent her frustration, she picked up the phone and rapidly punched out seven digits.

"Sarah? Roni. I certainly hope you've got that Save the Lambs rally nailed down for tonight. You have? Good. I've had it with those politicians.... What? Yes, don't I know it. Well, they won't be able to sweep *this* one under the rug, lambskin or otherwise, Sarah my friend. There'll be no more lamb chops or rack o' lamb on their plates, by golly, if *I've* got anything to say about it! Killing baby sheep—it's cruel! Sadistic! And every bit as disgusting as killing baby seals. Give a damn, save a lamb. Don't you love it? Right. I'll see you later, then...."

With a grim nod of satisfaction, Veronica dropped the phone into its cradle and rubbed her hands. She'd show these... "Cannibals," she said aloud.

"Another cause, pussycat?" Louise had come into the kitchen, unheard.

"You betcha." Full of purpose, Roni headed for the door to go look for materials to make a sign. "And a great one it is, too. They'll hear us all the way to the White House."

"Where've I heard *that* song before?" quipped Louise with a rolling of the eyes, though not before she was sure her niece was well out of earshot.

Hell couldn't be any hotter'n this!

Groaning, Gerald dropped an armful of two-by-fours on the ground, then straightened to wipe the sweat off his face with the rolled-up bandanna he had tied around his forehead. As he knotted it back in place, he took a moment to catch the breeze. The smell of new lumber overpowered the fragrance of summer flowers in bloom, but even so, the lungful of air was a treat. From behind, the whining screech and staccato bark of power saws and nail guns punctuated by shouts of profanity were a cacophony which made his ears ring and his head pound.

Construction. Gerald grimaced. When you were nothing but a lowly laborer, it wasn't a job for the timid and the weak.

He was neither, but, trudging back for another load of lumber, sweating in the hot sun and shaking his head in self-disgust, Gerald could almost hear Big Mike's voice jeering, "What the hell are you doin' there, you stupid jerk? Is *this* what I made you study for all them years, to break your back at a stinkin' job like *that?*"

Yeah, well. Gerald grimly compressed his lips. Big Mike wouldn't be telling him anything he hadn't been telling himself about fifteen times a day these past couple of weeks. And it wasn't as if he wouldn't rather be sitting in some cool, air-conditioned office listening to piped-in background music, designing mansions like this instead of blistering his hands helping to build them.

It was too soon, that's all. His past was still too much part of the present, his professional self-esteem and confidence still too fragile to be tested by rejection. Hell, why not be honest? He was scared. Scared that once he came nose-to-nose with prejudice and rejection, he'd toss everything he'd accomplished out the window and revert to form.

Only, this time he wouldn't just wind up with ten years snatched away. This time it'd be his whole life....

Just thinking about it had a fist of tension twisting his gut, so Gerald made himself stop thinking. It was a trick necessity had taught him many years ago, and it had stood him in good stead ever since. Just close up the brain cells; just *be*. Just *do*.

Checking his watch, he felt his spirits lighten. Quittin' time in fifteen minutes. Payday today—his first. He'd lasted two weeks at a regular job. Big Mike, locked away in that place till the end of his days and so adamant about making Gerald aim for something better, would be proud of that much, at least.

The weekend beckoned. Maybe he'd go look at some cars, kick a few tires. Time he got himself some wheels and stopped relying on that prickly landlady of his for favors.

He swore that damned woman could freeze a man at fifty paces!

And the hell of it was, it bothered him, the way her laughter vanished and her warmth turned to ice whenever he came near her or spoke to her. For some reason he wanted to see her smile just for him....

"Hey, Moose!"

The foreman's raucous voice startled Gerald out of his reverie.

"Sleep on your own time, will ya! Haul your butt and get them boards over here . . . !"

Great! Wonderful! A reason at last to show Gerald Marsden the door!

Her nerves strung so tight she felt sure any moment they'd pop like overwound violin strings, Roni paced. From the French doors to the old upright piano she'd tortured as a child, and back, with a fuming stop at the window in between.

So where *was* that no-good creep? It was ten to six. Why wasn't he home?

Onward to the piano. Turn. Toss a strained smile of reassurance at the silent visitor on the sofa while inwardly vowing to wring Marsden's neck and *then* toss him out!

Thank God Aunt Lou and the others were out. Given how upset *she* was with that good-for-nothing louse of a boarder and this unexpected state of affairs, it would surely kill Aunt Louise to learn that the nice young man she'd had such high—albeit unfounded—hopes for was nothing but a coward and a liar!

Footsteps! Roni flew to the window. *Aha!* For half a second she drank in the sight of him, even more torn than usual by the force of the conflicting emotions he made her feel, and then she grimly recalled herself.

With a hurried "Excuse me. Here he is now," she rushed from the room.

Gerald was only halfway up the walk when the front door of the boardinghouse flew open to reveal his disturbing landlady.

Just then, though, he noted the word *disturbed* would definitely be a more fitting description.

All legs and angles in short shorts and a T-shirt, she was charging toward him, breathing fire. *Now* what had gotten her dander up?

"Where have you been?" she demanded, planting herself squarely in his path and slamming fisted hands onto her hips. "Do you realize I've been waiting forever for you to show up?"

"Well, nooo..."

"You quit work at five. Then it takes you five minutes to gather your stuff, another ten to get home—"

"Hey, hold it!" Belatedly, his landlady's inexplicable and fishwifely reception lit Gerald's fuse. "What *is* this? Since when do I owe you an accounting of my time? I may eat and sleep here, lady, but I come and go as I please. Now if you'll excuse me!"

As he angrily shouldered past her, Roni noticed two bouquets of flowers in the hand he'd held hidden behind his back. For just an instant, she forgot her fury. Louise and Miz Henks would be so thrilled....

But then she remembered their visitor and saw red all over again. Rushing after him, she grabbed his arm. "Don't you dare set foot in that house until I've talked to you."

"Oh, yeah?" He easily shook her off. "Later, lady."

"Now, mister." She grabbed him again, hard.

He spun around, glaring. "Look, you, I'm hot and I'm tired and I'm getting damned fed up—"

"Well, so am I!" Veronica couldn't remember when she'd last been this enraged. "And you want to know why?" she spat. "Well, I'll tell you. You're a dirty rotten liar, Mr. Gerald Marsden, and if there's one thing I can't abide..."

Oh, God! Listening to Veronica's seething indictment with his guts twisting into an ever tighter knot, Gerald numbly thought, She knows. Somehow, she—*they* had found out.

" . . . it's a lying sneak. You told Aunt Lou you were on your own," Veronica heatedly accused, "but you're not, are you? You *do* have a family, don't you, you rotten louse? And you deserted them, didn't you, you, you . . . ?"

Aggravated beyond words, she punched the unyielding bulge of his bicep, then tightly hugged herself against the shivers of rage that shook her, and waited for him to say something in denial so that she could lambaste him some more.

But Roni's tirade had struck Gerald speechless. All he could do was stare at her and think, What? What? Why the hell was the woman ranting about his family?

"You are despicable, Mr. Marsden," Roni barked when Gerald just stood there, gaping. "And more than anything, I wish there was a way I could keep you away from that poor, neglected little boy . . ."

Boy?

"What boy?" Gerald finally managed to choke out. Thoroughly confused by Veronica's furious barrage of words and irrational demeanor, he seemed unable to grasp anything beyond the realization that he'd been granted a reprieve, that somehow his secret was still safe. As to all that other stuff . . .

Sweet Mother Murphy. His knees shook so bad, he dropped heavily on the steps. "I wish you'd tell me what the hell you're talking about."

"I'm talking about Peter Marsden. I'm talking about *your son!*" Veronica's voice was choked by the contempt that stuck like something vile and unswallowable in the middle of her throat and threatened to gag her.

To think that with the evidence sitting large as life inside her very house, the man would have the unmitigated gall to park his rump on her doorstep, look her in the eye and—

Oooh!

A renewed burst of fury gave Roni the strength to haul Gerald to his feet. "Get in that house, you despicable jerk. Go in there, look at that little boy and tell *him* you don't know who he is—if you dare.

"And then, Mr. Marsden," she concluded icily, "I want you to pack your stuff and *get out!*"

His head reeling, Gerald didn't resist as Roni roughly shoved him toward the door. His son? he kept thinking. Was the woman crazy? He had no wife. He had no children. He had no son.

So who the hell was Peter Marsden? No relative of his, that was for sure. He'd never even belonged to a family by the name of Marsden; the orphanage had hung that tag on him.

Stalking into the house with Veronica at his heels, Gerald tossed the flowers he'd bought for Lou and Miz Henks onto a mirrored credenza and came to a halt just inside the open French doors of the living room.

Eyes narrowed, he stared at his alleged son. And immediately thought, a little ruefully, that if his face looked only half as dark as his thoughts were, then no wonder the grubby little towhead sitting perched on the sofa was shrinking back against the cushions at the sight of him.

Hell. Wearily rubbing a hand across his face, Gerald struggled for calm and a less intimidating expression. He wasn't so angry that he enjoyed scaring little kids.

"Hi," he said, raising a couple of fingers in a sort of salute.

Nothing. The boy's only response was a frightened stare.

Dredging up a smile, Gerald went to hunker down in front of the boy. "So you're Peter, huh?"

The boy hesitated, then mutely nodded.

"They call you Pete or something?"

Watching Peter sort of half shrug, half nod, the boy's sullen wariness set off a chain of painful memories in Gerald. Hadn't he sat just so on many a strange sofa as a kid, being looked over and interrogated by adults none of whom had ever been the one he had most longed for?

Yeah, well... Rocking back on his heels, Gerald steeled himself against the surge of empathy. He wasn't what and who this kid might be longing for, that was for sure!

"So how old're you, Pete?"

Pete's barely audible "Five," was said with downcast eyes. They darted to the left once as Roni took a seat nearby.

Gerald looked at her, too, scowling, and thinking, *Five,* lady. D'you hear that? Five. I couldn't be this kid's father in a million years.

"Where's your mother?" he asked, any trace of burgeoning softness now buried beneath a mountain of frustrated resentment, most of it due to the fact that he couldn't come out and confront Miss High-And-Mighty Sykes with the irrefutable proof he had.

"I dunno."

"What's her name?"

"M-Mom."

"Who brought you here?"

"Nana."

"What's her other name? Her last name."

"Just Nana."

"Where's she live?"

Frustration was making Gerald impatient; there was an edge now to his voice that clearly frightened the boy and brought Veronica up on her feet.

"Gerald, could I see you in the hall a moment?"

So it was "Gerald" now, was it? Gerald shot her a black look, saw that she was distressed and thought, Well, tough, lady, so am I!

"No," he told her curtly, and once more addressed the boy, though in a more moderate tone. "Tell me where your nana lives, Pete, okay?"

The boy raised his eyes an instant. They were large, chocolate brown and quite at odds with his scruffy, flaxen hair and freckled face. Looking into them, Gerald had the fleeting sense that he knew someone else with eyes and hair like that, but the feeling was gone before he could really latch on to the image.

"B-Bisto," Peter said, looking down at his hands again. Hands, Gerald noted with a stab of something that made his throat painfully swell, that were small and dirty, and clutching the same kind of chocolate-chip-peanut butter cookie that had been in his own lunch box today.

The quick glance he tossed Roni was no longer quite so forbidding. "Don't you want to eat the cookie?" he asked the boy more gently still.

Peter's lips compressed, turning down at the corners, and his chin wobbled as he silently shrugged.

"Miss Sykes here makes the best, you know," Gerald went on, and as his gaze followed Peter's furtive glance to where Veronica stood, he saw that her expres-

sion held some of the same bewildered—and bewilder-
ing—tenderness that had suddenly put a scratchiness
into his voice. Obviously, this boy, so vulnerable, so
lost, was getting to her, too. "Aren't you hungry,
Pete?"

Another mute shrug. And a tear, dropping down on
the cookie.

"Gerald," Veronica said again, urgently. "I'd really
appreciate a word with you." And seeing Gerald's reluctance, quietly added, "Please."

Not waiting then if he was coming or not, Roni left
the room, leaving Gerald no choice but to follow or
seem totally boorish.

"Try the cookie," he told the boy, giving in to impulse and gruffly tousling his hair. "I'll be right back."

"That boy doesn't know you," Roni declared the
minute the door closed behind him.

"Gee, no kidding!"

Frowning intently, she ignored Gerald's heavy sarcasm. "And it's become obvious to me that you really
don't know who he is, and that you honestly don't think
you're his father...."

"Lady, I've got news for you. I don't just *think,* I
know I'm not that boy's father" was Gerald's angry
retort. "Is this all you dragged me out here to say?"

"No, but..." There was uncertainty now in Roni's
voice and expression. "What I mean is, how can you be
so sure? You're thirty years old. I'm sure you've been
around—" she blushed "—you know, *involved,* with
women. Couldn't it be possible—?"

"No. It couldn't."

"But—"

"I said no, dammit." Distraught, Gerald raked a hand through his hair, then dropped his arm with a sigh. "Look, I'm sorry, but you'll just have to take my word for it. It isn't possible, all right?"

But though he wished he could leave it at that and have it be enough, it was because Veronica kept looking at him so searchingly, and because he found for some reason that he wanted her to believe him and think well of him, that Gerald allowed her a glimpse of his past.

"See," he said grimly, "the thing is, I was abandoned by my own mother when I was only a few hours old and so you can take my word for it, I've always made totally damn sure I'd never leave a kid behind to be likewise tossed away."

Without sparing her another glance, he turned on his heel and would have ducked back into the living room, had not Roni's urgent "Wait" stopped him at the door.

"There's something else."

"What?"

"The elderly woman who brought Peter—"

Two steps took Gerald back to her. "You saw this woman?"

"Yes, I did, but—"

"And you didn't ask her name or where she lives?"

"No, darn it, but if you'll give me a chance to get a word in edgewise and explain . . ."

Stifling an oath, Gerald glared at the ceiling. "Go ahead, explain."

"She told me she couldn't stay—"

"I'll bet!"

" . . . but that you'd understand why she brought you the boy after you'd read her letter."

Gerald sharply exhaled, closing his eyes. "So where," he asked with hard-won patience, "is this letter, Veronica?"

Roni went to pick a dilapidated backpack up out of a corner. Wordlessly, she handed it to him.

Gerald saw the white envelope sticking out of the flapless front pocket and pulled it out. Dropping the pack, he ripped open the envelope and, after exchanging a quick, frowning glance with Veronica, perused the uneven script on the single page it contained.

Roni watched his lips thin as he read. His expression was grim but otherwise shuttered when he raised his eyes again to hers and, without speaking, passed the note over to her. She, too, perused it.

Dear Mr. Marsden,
You don't know me, but you knew my daughter
Marcy Kemp. She was Petey's mom. She was kilt
on a motorbike last year and left the boy with me
to raise. But, see, I can't do it no more. I got your
address in Oregon when I phoned Munson Is-
land...

Roni tossed a questioning glance at Gerald. "Munson Island?"

Gerald's mouth went dry. "That's in Maine. It's where I was for the last seven years." Swallowing, he added, "You familiar with it?"

Roni shook her head. "No."

Relief. Gerald was damn near shaking with it, but managed a careless shrug as he voiced the understatement of the century: "You haven't missed anything."

"Hmm." She was already reading again.

Marcy had the name of that place in with the boy's birth certificate. She told me to call you if things got tuff. She said you was her only friend and that you'd help me. So that's why I brung you the boy....

Roni lowered the letter. Looking at him, witnessing his distress, her heart softened in spite of her resolve to the contrary. "What can I say?"

"Nothing. There's more." Without looking at her, Gerald handed her the other sheet he'd been staring at.

Peter's birth certificate.

Roni's eyes immediately homed in on the name of the father—Last name, Marsden. First name, Gerald. Middle name, none—and lifted again to his.

"This says you're the boy's father."

"I know. But I'm not."

"But—"

"Dammit all!" Suddenly the secret he'd been so diligently guarding made Gerald feel like a cornered animal about to be trapped. He couldn't take it anymore. Hell, nobody should have to. He'd paid his debt....

Filled with rage, helplessness and despair, he slapped the palm of his hand against the wall, then spun to glare at Roni.

"You want to know why I'm sure?" he demanded, his tone all the more menacing for the harsh whisper it was. "Do you, huh?"

Frightened by his fierceness, Roni tried to back up a step.

But Gerald gripped her arm and held her in place. "You want to hear about Munson Island, Miss Sykes? Well, listen and I'll tell you...."

"No..." Roni was shaking her head, unwilling suddenly to hear whatever it was put that terrible look of pain and devastation into Gerald Marsden's blazing blue eyes. She wanted to cover his mouth with her hand to stop him from saying anything more and even half reached out to do it. But it was too late.

His voice hoarse and filled with despair, the words barely audible but clear, oh so clear, to Veronica, Gerald said, "Munson Island is a prison, Miss Sykes. It's a maximum-security federal penitentiary and I was inside of it for the last seven years."

Chapter Three

Roni stood as if turned to stone. Her incredulous gaze riveted to Gerald's. She was sure she had misheard him.

Prison...?

"W-what are you saying?" she finally managed to choke out. "That you're an ex— An ex—" She faltered.

"The word is ex-convict, Miss Sykes," Gerald said harshly. "And yes, that's what I'm telling you."

"B-but... What...?" Roni helplessly shook her head.

"Armed robbery. I was sentenced to ten years, seven of which I served. I was released on parole a couple of months ago."

Armed...robbery? Dear *Lord!*

Though she still didn't move physically, something inside Veronica jerked back in recoil from the picture of brutal violence Gerald's words conjured up—the picture of this man whom Aunt Louise and the others had trustingly welcomed into their home and hearts, pointing a gun at some hapless storekeeper's head and—

No. She closed her eyes to shut out the scene, to cut short the horrifying vision. Surely not. Surely they couldn't all have so thoroughly misjudged this man's character.

Watching Roni, seeing her shock, her revulsion, before she closed her eyes and didn't look at him anymore, something inside of Gerald died, something he hadn't even known had come alive.

"So now you know, Miss Sykes, don't you?" he said quietly. "Now you know why I'm so sure that Peter's not mine."

She didn't answer and, with a numbing coldness seeping into every cell of his body, Gerald turned and walked back into the living room.

There, the inadvertent initiator of this sorry chain of events had succumbed to the rigors of the day.

For long moments Gerald stood staring down at the little boy who, like a coil of rope, lay curled into himself, in the corner of the Upshots' shabby sofa, the uneaten cookie still clutched in his hand.

And he asked himself, What now?

Without a roof over his head—for there was no doubt in Gerald's mind that just as soon as Veronica recovered sufficiently from her shock to gather her wits, she'd be in here to show him the door—what was he going to do with a kid he neither knew nor wanted?

He was an ex-con, for cripe's sake. And before that for as long as he could remember, he'd been a kid alone and in trouble. What the hell did someone like him know about raising children—even if he were crazy enough to want to try? Which, it went without saying, he sure's hell wasn't.

Stymied, feeling helpless and trapped in a way he'd never felt before, not even in prison, Gerald jammed both fists into the back pockets of his jeans and heaved a sigh clear up from his toes.

What a mess!

Eyes burning, he stared down at the sleeping boy, taking in the fringe of lashes on freckled cheeks, the skinny little body in the too-big T-shirt, the scuffed knees, grubby hands and tattered runners.

And he knew a despair so heavy, his shoulders slumped from the weight of it, because suddenly he knew that there was no way he'd ever be able to do what common sense told him he should, namely to take this boy and deliver him into the hands of the authorities.

Yet, what were the alternatives? Find the grandmother? Sure. Gerald gave an inward, disgusted snort. A piece o' cake, right? All he'd have to do was figure out where the hell Bisto was and track down some old lady called Nana whose last name maybe was Kemp if she hadn't gone and married some guy called Jones or something....

Sweet Mother Murphy, what a mess!

Weary, itching from dried sweat and construction dust, Gerald tipped back his head and stared up at the ceiling. *Damn you, Marcy,* he thought. *How could you do this to me?*

And suddenly, as if in answer to his silent charge, there was another voice. A girl's voice. Marcy's...

"You're the only friend I ever had, Moose," she was saying, tagging her characteristic "You know?" at the end of the statement in that pathetic little-girl voice of hers.

She was visiting him in prison, just as she had pretty regularly all along, the only one of his crowd who

bothered. It must've been about his second year into the
sentence.

Thinking back, Gerald could remember protesting
her plaintive declaration with, "Hell, Marce, what're
you talkin' about? You got lotsa friends. All the
guys—"

"Want my bod," she'd cut in baldly. "They use me.
All except you."

"Yeah, well..." Discomfited because what she said
was true, and in spades, Gerald had shifted his gaze to
the guard who stood impassively nearby, and then on to
the row of men who, like himself, were talking through
a telephone to the visitors seated across from them behind a partition of bulletproof glass.

"I woulda let you, you know." Marcy's softly spoken words snapped his gaze back to hers. It was stark
with longing. "But you never asked."

Gerald had stared at her without speaking. What
could he say? That he'd never considered her in that
way? That in a life that was otherwise without scru-
ples, sexual fastidiousness had been—to him—impera-
tive? His one claim to decency?

Though it would be the truth to say so, not only
wouldn't she understand—how could she? He didn't!—
she'd be hurt. And keeping Marcy from getting hurt
had been his mission ever since the day she'd drifted
into the condemned building that Gerald and his cohorts had appropriated as their home.

Sixteen, a silver-blond, stereotypically cute California girl, Marcy had been like the little sister he'd never
had. And though he couldn't keep the others out of her
pants—not that she'd have wanted him to even try—he
had kept them from getting rough. In turn, Marcy had
become Gerald's shadow.

"I wish you didn't have to be in here," she was telling him now, laying the flat of her hand against the glass that separated them. Too thin, no longer sixteen, Marcy's fair-haired cuteness had long since been replaced by a hardened look of dissipation. "You didn't do nothin'."

"I held up a liquor store, Marce."

"But not with a gun, Moose! You never had no gun. 'Fact, I heard you say a million times, no weapons, no violence. It ain't smart...."

"Yeah." Gerald's laugh had been self-deprecatory. "Guess Joey and Sam didn't hear me though, did they?"

"But just because *they*—"

"Marcy." Sick of rehashing what he'd rehashed in his mind hundreds of times before, he'd cut short her futile protestations. "The bottom line is, a guy got shot and robbed and I was *there*. I was part o' the bunch who did it. As far's the law's concerned, that makes me as guilty as them. End of story, okay? Just forget it, will ya? I'm doing good."

"Are you? Really?"

"Yeah, I'm fine." They'd both been silent for a while then, with Gerald contemplating that particular falsehood, and Marcy apparently screwing up her courage to spit out what was on her mind this time.

Namely, "I'm pregnant, Moose."

Self-absorbed, he'd barely heard her. "What?"

She'd begun to cry. "I'm gonna have a baby."

"Aw, jeez!" He'd put the phone down and done some intense swearing. Calmer, he'd shaken his head at her, saying, "I guess you didn't listen to what I was telling you, either, Marce."

At her woeful look, he'd cussed some more, ending with "So you gonna get rid of it?"

"No!" She'd reared away from the partition as if slapped. "I was maybe thinkin' of going back to California, but I'd never—"

"Okay. Relax. I was just asking." Feeling helpless and hating it, furious with Marcy for being a slut and with himself for not having made her go home years ago, he'd blown air into his fist and glared at her. "Where the hell's the father anyway?"

Not meeting his eyes, Marcy had shrugged.

She didn't know.

"Hell, do you know *who* he is, Marce?"

Another shrug. She didn't know that, either.

And he'd thought disgustedly, That figures.

"I wish you were," she'd said, very quietly, after another long pause.

He'd rolled his eyes, snorting. "Yeah, right."

"I mean it, Moose. You're the greatest...."

You're the greatest.

Yeah. Sure. Gerald snorted in self-disgust, Marcy's accolade stinging like acid. He was so great that now, some six years later, standing in a boardinghouse thousands of miles from where that conversation had taken place and confronted with the baby she'd been so set to keep but, in the end, obviously couldn't, all he wanted was to find a way to get the kid off his own hands.

You're the greatest...

Feeling defeated and immeasurably tired, Gerald sank onto a hassock and buried his face in his hands.

The greatest...

He gave a short, bitter laugh. Oh boy, was he! The greatest loser, the greatest idiot. The greatest damned mess-up who ever lived.

Out in the hall, Veronica finally managed to drag her eyes off the French doors, which had shut behind Gerald Marsden with a decisive *click* several seconds earlier. Not sure what to do, how to act or even how to *re*act to Marsden's shattering revelations, she glanced at her watch.

Six-thirty. The others wouldn't be back from the card party and supper at the Senior Center for another couple of hours. Thank God for small mercies.

Roni glanced at the living room door again. Should she go in? But what could she do in there, what could she say? Just then she hardly even knew what to *think*.

She went into the kitchen. Shaded by the large maple in front of the window, the room was cool and dim. The smells of last night's corned beef and cabbage dinner still lingered. Unlike the day before, today had been too hot to cook, and with only Gerald and herself to feed, Roni had prepared a couple of salads to go along with leftover beef and some rolls.

Music, a classical piece featuring strings, issued softly from the small radio on the counter, but all Roni heard, over and over in her head were bits and pieces of Gerald Marsden's horrifying revelations. *I was abandoned by my own mother... only a few hours old... Munson Island is a prison... armed robbery... sentenced to ten years... I was abandoned... abandoned...*

Her movements slow and jerky, Roni sat down at her cluttered planning desk and stared at the small, fruit-and-flowers still-life print hanging above it. But instead of red-cheeked pears and luscious cherries, instead of sun-bright daisies and sky-blue forget-me-nots, she saw visions of a lost and lonely infant, toddler, child. And her eyes brimmed.

A sob welled up and she hung her head, tears dripping onto the desk as she imagined that child growing up, still unwanted, still lonely, still needy and trying to fill that need.

Stop it!

As if the command had been spoken aloud, Roni's head jerked up.

What're you doing? that same inner voice demanded. Marsden's a grown man, a criminal. Stop feeling sorry. Here's your chance! Kick the bum out!

Yes, but... Her gaze unfocused, Roni stared into the distance. He's trying to make a new start, she told herself. Here's your chance to do some real good. To give a man a second chance at life—could she think of a better cause than that? And to keep another little boy—Peter—from maybe following in that man's footsteps, wouldn't that be worth whatever effort it took?

Out in the hall the grandfather clock struck seven, bringing Veronica to her feet. Her movements sluggish with a weariness that was of the soul not of the flesh, she laid three place settings on the table, took the food she'd prepared out of the fridge and, after sparing another moment for a second thought, sighed and left the kitchen.

Her mind was made up. She would do all she could to help. After all, how could she, who had fought to save everything from whales, baby seals and lambs in her time, now turn her back on a needy man and child? She couldn't.

She entered the living room without knocking and stopped just inside the door, her ever-tender heart twisting at the sight of Gerald Marsden on the ottoman with his face in his hands. His head jerked up as soon as he heard her come in, but though he blinked the stark look of pain from his eyes almost instantly, Roni had seen.

Sensing that he wouldn't have wanted her to witness his unguarded moment of emotion, however, she took care to fix her concerned gaze on Peter and keep it there.

"He's all tuckered out, poor little guy," she said quietly, crouching down in front of the boy. "I've got dinner on the table," she added without turning. "It's a cold one, so there's no hurry, but I thought if you were hungry..."

Gently smoothing a lock of hair off the child's brow, she let the sentence hang. Behind her, she heard Gerald's knees creak as he got up from the low stool, and then footsteps as he walked to the window. Rising, too, she turned to look at his back. So imposing. So straight. And, just then, so very rigid.

"I'm sorry," she said, moving closer, but not crowding him. Gerald was sideways to her now and Roni could see his profiled features sharply defined against the light of the window. They looked as if carved out of rock, except for the tiny muscle tick just above his jaw. "I admit I was shocked by what you told me, but I've been doing some thinking."

"Have you."

"Yes. I've decided to let you stay. At least until you've sorted this mess out."

"Well." Roni saw Gerald's jaw clench before he relaxed it and slowly turned to face her. His expression was bitter. "That's mighty big of you, Miss Sykes."

"Yes, well..." She decided to ignore his sarcasm and took a deep breath. "I'd like to help if you'll let me."

"Would you now." Gerald stared at her as if she'd lost her mind. "Do you honestly think I didn't see how you felt about me out in that hall?"

"I told you, I was shocked. Who wouldn't be?"

"Who, indeed?" Gerald's lips thinned. "Not anybody I've ever met, that's for damn sure."

"Please..." Filled with an empathy she could not explain and chose not to examine, Roni raised her hand as if to touch his arm. Gerald moved out of reach before she could and she let the hand drop, saying, "There must be something I can do to make this easier for both of you...."

"I'm sure there is, Miss Sykes." He shifted his gaze to the floor, then, quizzically, brought it back up to hers. "The question is, why would you want to?"

Roni looked at the boy, so innocent in sleep. "For Pete's sake," she said simply, even if not quite honestly. Because the truth of it was, she found she very much wanted to help for Gerald's sake, too.

Chapter Four

Veronica Sykes had helped Gerald that evening in ways she couldn't even have begun to fathom. She had given practical help by serving—and actually getting Pete to eat—dinner, by taking care of sleeping arrangements for the boy and, when Louise and the boarders returned from their outing, by sketchily clueing them in without betraying any secrets he might not have wanted betrayed.

"What to tell them about your past, and when, is strictly up to you," she had told him. "And if you choose never to say a word, I'll respect that, too. They won't hear anything from me, that's a promise."

Gerald had been grateful for all she had done, of course, but it had been that promise, that entire declaration, that put him in her debt forever. Vulnerable and scared as he was, he'd desperately needed to hear those words even as he'd known he had no right at all to expect them. Her words, her promise, spoke of faith in him. Faith in his character, in his integrity. Faith that assumed—no, took for granted—that he, an ex-con who had done heavy time, could now be trusted to do the right and honorable thing.

How could he ever thank Veronica Sykes for that? How could he ever find the words to tell her how much her faith, her trust, her kind of help meant to him?

He couldn't. He didn't have the words any more than he had the courage to reach inside and search for them in the dark recesses of a soul he might or might not even have. You reached inside and groped around, and God only knew what kinds of stuff you were liable to drag out into the light of day and for all to see. And then it would be so easy to get hurt. . . .

Staring up at the ceiling, mottled by a pattern of moonlight filtering through the lace curtain at his window, Gerald listened to the faint, unfamiliar sounds of the kid's breathing—Pete was bedded down on a cot in Gerald's room—and he knew that getting hurt was already a very real possibility.

Because already he found himself worrying if the boy was warm enough in that cot, and thinking of things he could teach him and show him and share. All the things he'd missed out on as a kid, he found himself tempted to give and do for this boy who wasn't even his. And so he'd better take care, he'd better be very careful, because if he wasn't, if he got attached to the boy and used to having him around, then how was he gonna feel when it came time to give him back?

And he *had* to give him back. There was no way he could keep him. He wasn't the father of that boy.

Hell. Gerald punched his pillow and grimly rolled over so that his back was toward the room and Pete's cot. He didn't want to be a father at all.

* * *

As a rebellious and angry teenager, Veronica had avoided like the plague heart-to-heart talks with her Aunt Louise. But now, at twenty-six, she had no such qualms. In fact, for quite a number of years now, she and Louise treasured their occasional nocturnal exchanges of gossip, trivia and confidences as special times neither one of them would want to miss. They weren't regularly scheduled events—no appointments were made or signals given—they just happened.

Something would come up, or maybe *nothing* would seem to ever be happening, whatever. Come eleven o'clock or so, with everyone else safely retired, Roni's door would creak open and, nightshirted and robed, she'd tiptoe across the hall to Louise's room where she'd make herself comfortable against the footboard of her aunt's old-fashioned bed with her feet snuggled beneath the quilt, and then they'd talk.

Tonight was no different, except that for quite a little while the two women merely sat and contemplated each other in pensive silence.

"I'm proud of you, pussycat," Louise finally said. "You handled that scared little boy like a pro."

"Well, I *am* a teacher."

"So's Dick Harrison, but that hasn't made him warm and caring, now has it?"

"Hardly," Roni conceded with a little chuckle. Harrison was a friend, a math teacher and basketball coach with a hard-nosed drill-sergeant manner.

"You handled our Gerald pretty well, too," Louise continued. "Seems to me, he's a very troubled young man."

Making no reply—what could she say? Lou was right—Roni bit her cheek and looked down at her fingers, worrying the quilt. She wished she could confide in her aunt about Gerald's violent past, maybe ask her counsel. It was why she'd come, she realized now. But, being here, she knew she couldn't say a word. She'd promised Gerald she wouldn't, and that was that. But she was troubled, and so darn unsure.

Had she done the right thing, telling him he could keep on living here at the boardinghouse, without first talking it over with Louise and the others? Their lives would be as negatively impacted as her own, should Gerald fail to live up to the faith she'd decided— blindly—to place in him.

And little Peter. Again, should she not have consulted the other members of the household before allowing him—a young child—to become a part of it, too? Old Mrs. Henks had never had children and she'd never made a secret of her aversion to them, either. How was she going to feel about having a little boy underfoot for who knew how long?

"I don't know, Aunt Lou . . ." Roni looked up with a sigh. "Did I do the right thing?"

"About what?"

"Letting them stay. . . ."

"Well, o' course you did, sweetheart. Where else were they gonna go? The others agree, by the way."

"Well, that's a relief anyway." Eyes back on the fingers that compulsively rolled and unrolled the comforter's edge, Roni frowned. "But even so, I can't help but wonder—"

"Explain to me again how Gerald's not the boy's father," Louise interrupted. "I mean, why would a woman saddle a man with her kid unless he was some rich guy she's hopin' to hold up for support?"

"Well . . ."

"I mean, Gerald doesn't have a pot to pee in and, by the looks o' the stuff he brought with him, never had one, neither. It doesn't make sense."

"Since when do relationships have to make sense?" Roni said, hoping to sidestep the issue. "And anyway, it wasn't the mother who brought the boy, it was—"

"The grandma, I know. But she's not the one who stuck Gerald's name on that birth certificate."

"That's true." Shifting, Roni tucked her feet up under her. And since Marcy Kemp was safe territory, she added, "Gerald told me that Peter's mother was originally from California. You ever hear of a town called Bisto there, Aunt Lou?"

"Bisto?" Louise frowned. "Sure you're not thinkin' Frisco, hon?"

"'Course I'm sure." Roni shot her a wryly reproving glance. "The two don't even sound alike. And anyway, Petey said he and his nana lived in Bisto."

"Hmm."

"Right." Pulling a face, Roni nodded. "Could be anywhere." She paused, choosing her words carefully so as not to betray any confidence. "Gerald also told me that this Marcy Kemp person was, well, let's just say she was *friendly* with a lot of guys—"

"You mean she slept around."

Trust Lou not to mince words. Roni shot her aunt another wry glance. "Yes. But she was *friends* only with Gerald," she continued soberly. "Platonically. He says he, uh, looked out for her and she, well, it seems she loved and respected him for it."

Louise snorted derisively. "Some way to show love and respect, sticking a man with a kid that's not his."

Roni regarded her aunt with lips compressed, thoughtful. "I know this might sound weird," she finally said, "but *I* think that's exactly what Marcy Kemp was trying to do by naming Gerald Marsden as her child's father—show her love and respect.

"I wonder if Gerald's looked at it that way," she continued more to herself, frowning. "Hmm..."

The women were silent a moment as each pursued their own thoughts. And then Louise said, "Still mad at me now for renting him the room, pussycat?"

Roni glanced up at her aunt with a puzzled frown. Her thoughts had been on ways in which she might help to ease both the man and the child into a mutually rewarding relationship. "What d'you mean?"

"You were so dead set against him...."

"Ufff..." went Roni, expelling air as she dismissed her aunt's assertion with a gesture of impatience. "I knew what you were up to, that's all."

"Up to?" asked Louise, innocently. "Up to what?"

"No good," Roni countered, "that's what. Matchmaking or whatever you want to call it. You know how I hate that, Aunt Lou. I mean, if I wanted to meet men, don't you think I'd go out and meet them? I sure's heck would not wait around for you and your cohorts to haul 'em in off the streets, for heaven's sake."

"Worked, though, didn't it?" said Louise smugly. "You're sitting here worrying about him, aren't ya? And only a couple weeks after you said you wanted no part of 'im."

Lord, give me a break, Roni thought, exasperated. "I swear, you've got a one-track mind, Aunt Louise. Wanting to help out when a guy has the kind of problems Gerald's got right now is hardly 'wanting a part of him' in the way that you're talking about, for crying out loud. It's simple human decency, that's all."

"Next, you'll be telling me he's just another of your causes."

"All right." Roni shrugged, pretending indifference. "He's just another one of my causes."

"If you say so."

Lord, but the woman could be exasperating! Irked by her aunt's amused skepticism, Roni flared, "Yes, I do say so. And as to being against his moving in here in the first place, it wasn't so much *him* I was mad at, it was *you.* And the others, I might add. All of you know darn good and well I can't *stand* to be manipulated like that. And I thought I'd made it perfectly clear that I like my life just fine the way it is."

"But it's unnatural, child!" Louise reached across the bed and caught Veronica's hand. "I can remember when you were a little girl, playing house with your dolls, playing wedding with that old curtain draped over your head for a veil and dragging poor Ralphie Lieberman up the garden path. You always wanted to get married, Roni, and you should. You love kids—it's why you became a schoolteacher...."

"But I don't teach much anymore, do I?" Roni countered. "People change, Aunt Lou. Wishes change...."

"Baloney. Yours didn't change until after we started up the boardinghouse."

"Right," Roni said with finality, knowing full well if she didn't put a stop to this futile discussion, Louise would keep riding the subject ad infinitum, it being her favorite hobbyhorse. "So what do I need with a husband and children to drive me insane when I've got you and the others to do it, instead? Right?" She withdrew her hand from her aunt's loose clasp and with a sharp nod, added, "Of course, right."

"Wrong."

Roni rolled her eyes. "Aunt Lou—"

"No, listen to me," Louise interrupted. "Somethin' just sunk into my dense old noggin' here." She tapped her head, glaring at her niece. "You don't want to get married because of *us?*"

"Well..."

"Well *what,* for crying out loud? Yes or no?"

Roni shrugged, frowning. "Well, yes, in a way. I mean, who'd look after all of you—"

"Who cares?" Louise exclaimed.

"*I* care." Roni rubbed her forehead; a headache threatened. She had not wanted to get into any of this tonight. Or ever, for that matter. She'd made up her mind about it all more than three years ago when—

"Does this have to do with Scott Miller?" Louise asked sharply.

"I don't—"

"Don't play cute with me, missy." She leaned forward and pinned Roni against the backboard with her eyes. "Now I want the truth. Were we the reason you called off your engagement to Scott?"

Roni sighed, the headache no longer a threat but full-fledged reality. "Partly," she grudgingly allowed.

"Care to elaborate, young lady?"

Aunt Lou was mad, that much was clear. And Roni knew better than to prevaricate and evade when Louise was in a snit. Still, she tried. "It's all such ancient history, Aunt Lou. What—"

"Veronica Sykes...!"

"Oh, all right," Roni said crossly. "Scott had a job lined up out of state and I told him there was no way I'd leave the boardinghouse. End of story." She glared at her aunt. "You happy now?"

Louise didn't look happy. Quite the contrary, she looked crushed. And, for long moments, she seemed to have been struck speechless. At length she closed her eyes, her lips set in a straight, grim line. Slowly she began to shake her head. And when she opened her eyes again to look at Roni, they were bright with moisture.

"Oh, Veronica..." was all she said, but with such sorrow, that tears stung Roni's eyes, too. And, with a muffled cry of dismay, she scooted across the bed and embraced her aunt.

"Aunt Lou," she beseeched, "please don't do that. It doesn't matter...."

"Oh, but it does." Louise covered her eyes with one hand. "It does."

"Noooo. Listen." Roni pulled away her aunt's hand so she could look her in the eye. "It's much better this way. Really. I realized quite some time ago that I never loved Scott. I couldn't have. I mean, after we broke up, did you ever see me cry about it?"

"No, but—"

Roni stopped her aunt's words with her finger. "And didn't he get married only four months later?" At Lou's nod, she said, "Well, then, there you are. He never really loved me, either. Now—"

Roni straightened. "I'll say this just one time and then we'll drop the subject forever. Okay?"

Louise looked doubtful, but nodded. "Shoot."

"You and the others are my family. Hush, now, *I'm* talking," she said when her aunt drew a breath to interrupt. "I love every one of you and I don't ever want to leave you."

"But, Roni—"

"No, Aunt Louise. I know what you want to say, that sooner or later all of you will leave me. But—" she hurried on to forestall another interruption "—not all at once, and somebody else'll move in here to take their place and for me to care for. I'm probably weird, but I happen to really like old people—''

"You're weird, all right." This, fondly, from her aunt.

"And I really like doing what I'm doing, and I want to keep on doing it. The only way I could ever see myself getting married would be if the man'd be willing to move in here with all of us. As far as I'm concerned, we're a package deal, Aunt Lou. All or nothing.''

Roni kissed her aunt and gave her a loving smile, which grew ruefully philosophical as she added, "And since there's not a lot of men out there willing to go with those terms . . .'' She shrugged. *"C'est la vie.''*

"What's that mean?''

"Means, who needs 'em anyway.'' Roni scrambled off the bed, stretched and yawned. "Lord, I'm tired. . . .''

It seemed to Veronica she'd only just gone to sleep when a soft knock on the door roused her to instant alertness. One of the boarders was sick!

"Coming.'' Grabbing up her robe, still in the process of slipping it over the football-jersey-type nightshirt she wore, she rushed to open the door—only to find herself facing a very distraught Gerald Marsden across the threshold.

"I'm sorry,'' he whispered, not so upset he didn't notice the surprisingly alluring picture Roni made with her tousled dark mane and sleepy face, and those miles of shapely bare legs. "I hate to wake you, but. . .''

"What is it?'' Roni could hardly get the words out as any last remnants of sleepiness were zinged away by the heart-stopping proximity of Gerald Marsden's bare torso. Massive, tanned, every muscle clearly defined, it was sprinkled with just the right number of curly golden hairs for a woman to comb her fingers through....

Roni was chagrined by the effort it took to lift her gaze to his face, and by how breathless she sounded as she asked, "What's wrong?"

"It's the boy." He shouldn't have come here, Gerald thought. "He's making noises..." Seeing Veronica like this was stirring up longings he didn't want stirred. He backed up a step. "I...I'm sorry." Backed up another. "I guess it's nothing. I... Good night, Miss Sykes."

Good night, Miss Sykes?

"Wait a minute. Hold it." Roni stepped out into the hall, frowning. "You mean, Peter is crying?"

"Not really." A final backward step brought Gerald flush against the wall across from her door. He was stuck. "More like, you know—whimpering."

"I'm going to go see." Roni was already hurrying toward the stairs.

"No, don't." In moments she'd be in his room. Right by his bed. Though she was in there every week, cleaning and changing the bed linens, now suddenly it seemed too intimate. "It's okay, I—"

She wasn't even listening and, with a muttered curse, Gerald let it drop and went after her. Fine time to be getting cold feet anyhow. And damn the kid for getting him into this mess. What was he crying for, anyway? *He* wasn't the one saddled with responsibilities he neither wanted nor knew how to handle!

No, but he's been dumped in a strange house with strange people and another grouchy stranger who's supposed to be his father. In his shoes, wouldn't you cry, too?

Yeah. Feet dragging as he followed Roni into his room, Gerald released an explosive sigh and stood rubbing the back of his neck as Veronica perched on the edge of Pete's cot and solicitously bent over the child.

"Hush," she murmured, "hush, little Petey." She gently brushed the boy's hair off his forehead, all the while crooning tender little nothings that nevertheless seemed to soothe and quiet the boy.

Watching her, thinking of all he'd missed as a child— was missing even now—emotion surged painfully into Gerald's throat. Love, hate, yearning, denial and anger—always that terrible anger—were all mixed together in a lump so large, he could neither swallow it nor spit it out.

His mother. Man, but he hoped she was rotting in hell.

Because where had she been when he'd cried himself to sleep more nights than he cared to remember? Where had she been when he'd nearly died from meningitis and had called for her? Where had she been when he'd been cold and hungry and alone on the streets, not much older than this boy, and trying to survive as best he could?

Where had she been? Why hadn't she wanted him? Why hadn't she loved him?

Why hadn't anybody *ever* loved him?

"Gerald?" He was staring at her so strangely, Roni thought. So... angrily.

"What?"

And he sounded angry, too.

Getting up off the cot, she went to him. But standing closely before him, it wasn't anger she saw in his shadowed gaze, but a pain so raw, she had to stifle a gasp of reaction and an almost overwhelming urge to reach out and comfort him as she had comforted little Peter.

"I know how difficult this is for you," she said softly, feeling inadequate yet aware that they didn't know each other well enough for the kind of comforting gesture she longed to make.

"Do you?" The woman might mean well but she knew squat, Gerald thought bitterly. All her life she'd had the kind of love, warmth and security he and little Pete over there could only dream about. And cry about.

He and little Pete...

The phrase stuck, jarring him, shaking him up. He and Pete. Kinship. Not of the blood, of course, but even so. In many ways they were alike, he and Pete. And in this room, tonight, it wasn't he who was the odd one out, it was she. Veronica.

"Thanks for coming up here to check on the boy," he told her stiffly. "Sorry I woke you."

"Don't be silly..." Pulling her robe tightly around herself and holding it like that by crossing her arms and gripping her elbows, Roni tamped down a surge of hurt at Gerald's change in attitude. The man had an awful lot on his plate right now, she reminded herself, and the Lord only knew what demons from the past he was dealing with, to boot. The last thing he needed was for her to play the injured maiden.

"I think he'll be fine now," she said, moving toward the door as Gerald stepped aside to let her pass. "If not, please don't hesitate—"

"I'll manage."

"I'm sure you will." She tried for a smile. "Good night, Gerald."

"G'night."

* * *

Saturday breakfasts at the boardinghouse were always elaborate affairs. None of this toast and cereal stuff, or plain old bacon and eggs. Those things might do on Sundays or during the week, when either work, scheduled activities or church demanded a speedier meal and punctuality. Saturdays it was stacks of syrupy pancakes, or sausage and strawberry waffles, or omelets with everything in them but the kitchen sink.

Today it was pancakes. With the exception of Gerald and the boy, everybody was assembled around the large kitchen table, sipping juice and coffee while commenting on how none of them had heard as much as a peep out of the little fella all night.

"He'll be no trouble," Aunt Louise decreed, her expression daring old Miz Henks to say otherwise.

Mrs. Henks, not unexpectedly, promptly did. "It's early times yet," she said primly. "I've had plenty of six-year-olds in my library in my time—"

"Boy's five."

"—and let me tell you, they're noisy little rascals, every one."

"Boys'll be boys," said Leo.

"'Course, there're boys and then there're boys." This from Judge Cunningham. "Why, I've handled cases—"

"Judge, you won the coin toss," Roni interrupted what could easily turn into one of the judge's lengthier dissertations on preadolescent criminality. "Come get your pancakes. Miz Henks, you're next."

Roni had two griddles going, and was busily flipping, stacking and pouring batter.

"Aunt Lou, why'nt you go see what's keeping—"

"Good morning."

Gerald came into the kitchen, his freshly showered good looks momentarily derailing Roni's train of thought. "Oh," she finally said, collecting herself. "Hi. There you are. Have some juice or milk and I'll pour some more batter on the grid—"

"The boy won't come out of the bathroom."

"What?"

"Won't come out of . . . ?"

"What's the matter . . . ?"

Everybody was talking at once, with Mrs. Henks smugly saying, "See? Trouble already. Didn't I tell you . . . ?"

And Aunt Lou, tut-tutting sympathetically, "Poor little tyke, he's scared."

"I told him to go in there and wash up," Gerald said to Veronica above the hubbub the boarders were causing. "And now he won't come out."

She stared at him, smelled something burning, swore and hurriedly turned some pancakes. "What'd you do to him?"

Gerald's eyebrows lowered, his chin shot out. "What d'you mean?"

Roni, heaping the judge's and Mrs. Henks's plates, bit her lip and warned herself to tread softly. "I only meant, if you go around glaring at Pete the way you're glaring at me right now, no wonder he's hiding."

So much for treading softly.

"I didn't say he's hiding, and I'm not glaring." What Gerald was doing was *scowling*. "All I told him was he'd better step lively or no breakfast."

"Swell." Tossing him a speaking glance which loudly said, "You blew it, Mac," Roni served Leo and her aunt and poured more batter onto the griddle.

"Here," she said, handing Gerald the spatula. "Look after these while I go talk to Peter. Don't burn 'em," she warned, already halfway out the door. "They're yours."

She met the little boy halfway up the stairs and they both stopped moving, a couple of steps apart, when they spotted each other.

"Well, hi there, Pete," Roni said brightly. She was below him by two steps which made them almost eye level to each other. It was pretty obvious that whatever else Peter might have done in that bathroom, washing and combing hadn't been part of the activity. Crying, however, very definitely seemed to have been, Roni noted with a wrench. Fresh tracks of moisture were evident on his grubby little face. "I was just coming to see if you needed help or anything in the bathroom."

Pete compressed his lips and shot her a sullen look, but didn't say anything.

Roni held her hand out to him, saying, "Guess I should've known a big boy like you can wash all by himself. You did wash?"

When Peter peered up at her again, she smiled encouragingly. He shook his head and whispered, "Couldn't."

Roni digested that a moment, then pulled a face, slapping the palm of her hand against her forehead. "Of course you couldn't," she exclaimed. "Now what's the matter with me? I'll bet you needed a footstool, didn't you? Those darn taps are too high for a kid to reach."

Climbing abreast of him, all the while talking, Roni matter-of-factly took the boy's hand and reversed his direction. "I used to have the same problem when I first came to live here as a kid. My Uncle George fixed me right up. Say. . ." She stopped to regard him with eyes wide. "Have you ever been in a treasure attic?"

Peter hesitantly shook his head, still shy, but Roni was gratified to see that the sullenness had been replaced by a spark of interest.

"I thought not," she said and, tugging him along to the end of the upstairs hall, opened a small door. "Well, get a load o' this, my boy. . ." She pulled a string on a lightbulb and stepped aside, delighted to note that curiosity had now completely overcome Peter's shyness. "These're all my old toys," she told him, rummaging around for the footstool George had built for her twenty years ago. "Lucky for you I liked trucks and stuff just as much as I liked my dollies. If you want, after breakfast you and, uh. . ."

She faltered, not sure whether to say, your dad, your father, Gerald or what. "And your, uh—"

"Hey, what're you two up to in there?" a male voice suddenly questioned from behind them.

Roni started and wheeled around to see Gerald's imposing breadth fill the doorway while Peter guiltily dropped the shiny red musical top he'd been admiring. He hid his hands behind his back as if expecting to get them slapped.

"She said I could," he mumbled, eyes on the floor.

Roni's heart went out to him. Her eyes meeting Gerald's in mute communication, she dropped down beside the boy and, clasping an arm around his shoulders, hugged him to her encouragingly.

"Are they sending search parties out looking for us?" she asked cheerily. Anything to show the boy that Gerald's gruffness need not intimidate. Rising, she took Peter's hand in hers, picked up the stool and gently urged him toward the door.

"We needed to find this young man here something to stand on so he can get at the sink and wash, didn't we, Petey?" She caught Gerald's eye again and held it, sending a message that said, Take it easy with the kid. "And I was showing Peter where there's toys and stuff for him to play with later."

Gerald stepped back out into the hall and they followed. "That attic was always my favorite place to hang out on a rainy day," Roni said, steering Pete into the bathroom, setting down the stool and turning on the taps.

"Today's a rainy day," Peter said.

"Why, so it is." Roni, handing him a washcloth, shot a triumphant glance at Gerald hovering out in the hall. Peter had spoken a whole sentence. She reached for a towel to dry his face. "Lucky you. Where is your comb, Gerald?" she asked.

His comb?

"We need to tame the mop on this kid," Roni elaborated, and to Peter she said, "Later you can go buy a comb of your own. You can pick out the one you want."

She glanced at Gerald who was looking about as sullen and uncertain as Peter had earlier while he yanked open a drawer and handed her a comb. "How'd that be, uh..."

Dad, she'd wanted to say again, but there was nothing in Gerald's expression to indicate he'd welcome the appellation and so she left the question as it was.

A surge of emotion stung her eyelids, however, when both man and boy betrayed their anxieties by simultaneously asking, "Will you come with us to the store?"

Chapter Five

Considering his former shyness and his lack of appetite the night before, Peter astounded the women and delighted the elderly men by putting away seven butter-and-syrup-dripping pancakes and two glasses of milk. He raked up considerably more brownie points by afterward inviting the judge and Leo up to the attic with him.

They went most willingly to look at treasures with him while Aunt Lou and Mrs. Henks piled into the Senior Center's van for a much anticipated shopping expedition to a nearby outlet mall.

This left Gerald and Roni alone to finish their coffee.

They sat in silence—it was not a companionable one—each staring down into their cups. Both had several things they would have liked to say to the other, but neither seemed able to find a—to them—suitably innocuous opening.

"Good pancakes," Gerald finally remarked into his cup.

"Thanks." Roni glowed far more than the compliment merited.

"All your food's really good, you know." Gerald half stretched, and patted his midsection as his eyes sort of slid to hers with an abashed little grin. "I'll bet I've put on a pound or two."

Of their own accord, Roni's eyes caressed his torso. Every well-developed muscle was tantalizingly defined beneath his formfitting T-shirt and there wasn't a spare pound in sight. "I doubt it."

Their gazes bounced off each other's once again, like butterflies too skittish to linger. Gerald's settled back on his coffee. He'd put too much cream in it. Nerves. He cleared his throat, struggling to get past whatever was keeping him from giving expression to what he was feeling inside.

"I, uh...*ah-hum*—"

Damn frog. Gerald scowled, took a sip of his too-white coffee, almost choked on it and coughed some more. Deep breath.

"I, er, just want you to know that I . . ." He faltered again, raised his eyes and inadvertently let Roni catch a glimpse of the struggle inside.

A surge of something almost maternal made her want to stroke his cheek and say, It's all right. Don't be afraid. Spit it out. Her smile of intended encouragement wasn't quite steady.

"Damn." She was looking at him the way she probably looked at her students at school, and he was feeling about eight years old, too. All tongue-tied and awkward. Disgusted with himself, Gerald shook his head and expelled a harsh breath. "I guess I want to say thank you, but I can't seem to... you know..."

"Well, that's good." Pushing back her chair, Roni rose, using briskness to cover up how touched she was by Gerald's struggles for eloquence. "Because there's nothing to thank me for. I enjoy cooking—" She knew darn well her cooking wasn't under discussion here, but aside from being uncomfortable with gratitude, she wanted to spare Gerald further discomfiture. "—and you're paying good money for the meals you get."

But Gerald refused to accept the easy out she offered. The things she'd done for him these past couple of days went way beyond what anybody else would've done, and he wanted her to know he appreciated it. Getting up, too, he joined her at the sink. She kept on rinsing and stacking dishes and Gerald began loading them into the dishwasher. It was the first time he'd ever helped out like that, and he did so now without consciously thinking about it. Performing the chore seemed to release the mental word jam.

"I'm well aware, you know," he said, deftly sorting cutlery into the rack in the dishwasher door, "that you didn't want me in this house at first. No," he said, forestalling the protest Roni's abrupt inhalation told him she wanted to make. "It's okay. Because what I want to say is, it makes me appreciate even more the way you're handling all this stuff I've been dumping on you here."

"Gerald—"

"No, let me get this said, okay?" They were face-to-face now, their hands idle. "I'm an ex-con, Veronica. I did hard time for what they call a crime of violence. Most people—"

"You'll find that when things get right down to it, I'm not like 'most people,'" Roni interrupted quietly.

"I already know that." He regarded her steadily, no longer unsure of his feelings and words, and saw that her striking green eyes were serious, her cheeks flushed from her morning's labors at the griddle and from the heat of the sudsy water in which her hands were still submerged. And he noted with mild surprise that just then, all rosy and with her hair mussed, Veronica Sykes looked almost pretty.

He realized that he was growing to really like this landlady of his, and gave her a smile. "But as I said, anyone else finding out that the guy they didn't want in their house in the first place was a criminal, they'd have him out on his ear so fast it'd make his head spin. You didn't do that—"

"Don't pin any wings on me, Gerald." Roni felt herself growing flustered by the intensity of his regard. "I'm no angel and I won't pretend I was happy about Louise renting you the room."

"You were royally ticked, is what you were."

"Well, maybe." Roni colored. Disconcerted by the warmth of his gaze and the husky mellowness of his voice, she tore her gaze from his and looked down at her heat-reddened hands in the sink. "But I told you why, too."

"Matchmaking?"

"That's right." Roni's face grew hotter. "I guess I shouldn't have let it upset me, and ordinarily it wouldn't have, but in your case—"

She abruptly stopped talking when she realized what she'd been about to admit, and cast him a quick sideways glance.

He was eyeing her quizzically, one brow arched. "What about in my case?" he prompted.

And Roni suddenly thought, What the heck, and defiantly faced him. "But in your case," she said, raising her chin, "it did upset me because you're so much better looking than any of the others they've stuck me with, that I almost hated them."

"But why, for crying out loud?" Gerald said after a long pause during which their gazes seemed to get sort of tangled up.

"Because..." A little wistfully, Roni shrugged. "I mean, *look* at me...."

Gerald's gaze softened. "I *am* looking...."

Which was when sanity mercifully returned and Roni, with an embarrassed little laugh, managed to swing her gaze back into the dishwater. "Yes, well," she said dryly, hoping her galloping heartbeat wouldn't be too discernible in the pulse at her throat. "Most men don't."

And then quickly, before Gerald got the idea that maybe she wanted him to protest or something, she laughed again and exclaimed, "Good grief—how'd we get so maudlin all of a sudden, anyway? Here, see if you can find a spot for this bowl, will you?"

It would have taken an insensitive dummy not to realize Roni wanted the subject dropped. Since Gerald didn't consider himself either of those, he swallowed the polite disclaimer he'd been about to make and, stowing the mixing bowl she'd handed him, said, "We were discussing those pesky boarders."

"Right." Her grateful glance made him glad he'd been tactful. "They can be a royal pain now and then."

"I'll bet." Gerald stowed another couple of forks she'd unearthed and straightened. "Though I don't mind telling you, I'm glad to be one of their number. There's not too many places like this here in town."

"Boardinghouses are old-fashioned." Roni took the sink stopper out and swirled her rag around to make the suds go down with the water. "In fact they're fast becoming extinct. Certainly there's not much call for them with people our age." She cast him a glance, saying, "I'm twenty-six," in an explanatory aside.

"I'm thirty."

Roni acknowledged that with a nod while Gerald wondered why he'd said it.

"After parental homes and college dorms," Roni went on as she rinsed the sink with clean water, glad to be on safe conversational ground again, "all the people my age that I know want places of their own with roommates, housemates, playmates..."

"How come *you* don't?"

Gerald's softly voiced question stilled Roni's hands. Keeping her gaze on them, after a long silence she said, just as quietly, "Who says I don't?"

Later, in her room and changing into a comfortable denim skirt and checkered blouse for the shopping trip with Pete and Gerald, Roni still couldn't believe she had actually said that. Until the words were out of her mouth, she hadn't even known she'd felt that way but, once said, she'd recognized them as the truth.

Everything else, all the reasonable, rational rhetoric she had always so volubly spouted on the subject had been just that—rhetoric. Pretty speeches with which to convince Aunt Louise, the boarders...and herself. And they'd worked; they'd all bought it, when the truth was Uncle George had died and there'd been no money to go away to college or anything else. End of story. Period.

She'd earned her teaching degree by first attending a local community college and afterward completing her third and fourth years at Willamette University with the help of scholarships while living at home. Taking in boarders was the only way they'd been able to keep the house, but Louise alone would never have been able to manage. And so Roni had stayed, first to help and, gradually, to take charge and run things.

The scary part was, Roni thought, brushing her hair without looking at her reflection in the mirror, that until about an hour ago she'd believed herself perfectly happy and content. She slowly lowered the brush and forced herself to meet the sober green gaze of her mirror image.

What else have you been fooling yourself about, Roni Sykes?

"Will you look at that now, Pete my boy," Judge Cunningham boomed from the back seat of Roni's car where he and the boy were ensconced. "There's a small carnival set up in the shopping center parking lot with a Ferris wheel and all. I'll bet if you ask your dad very nicely—"

"I don't got a dad."

"Why, sure you do, boy!" the judge exclaimed. "Why, he's right there in front of you." Whatever his thoughts about the situation—along with Louise, he and the others had only been sketchily filled in the previous evening—the judge's only reaction to the boy's truculent statement was cheerful bluster.

"You need glasses or something?" he joshed, giving his little seatmate a playful dig in the ribs with his elbow. "What are you, kid, blind? You look just like the man—"

"Do not."

"Why, you even got muscles like him! Hard as a rock." The old man poked Peter's bicep but couldn't make him smile. "'Course if you're scared to ride a Ferris wheel..."

"I'm not scared o' nothin'."

"You're not?!"

"Uh-uh." Pete shot a nervous glance at Gerald who had turned around to frowningly study the boy. "My nana even said."

"Hmm." Judge Cunningham pursed his lips as if thinking. "And what else did your nana say?"

"Not to talk to strangers."

"Aahh..." The old man nodded approvingly.

"Are you a stranger?" asked Pete.

"Me...?" Judge Cunningham drew back as if offended. "Of course not. I'm your friend. Didn't I help you make a fort in the attic and everything?"

Peter nodded, though a little uncertainly.

"And don't I live in the same house with you?"

Another nod. A bit more conviction.

"Well, then, I'd say that makes me your friend, wouldn't you?"

"We're your friends, too, Pete. Gerald and I." Roni caught the boy's eye in the rearview mirror and, smiling, gave him a wink. "That's why Nana brought you to us, you know. Isn't that right, Gerald?"

Gerald, his expression much like Peter's sullenly doubtful one, didn't reply right away. He was smarting from Peter's earlier rejection of him as his father, though why the hell that should bother him he had no idea. After all, he didn't want to be the kid's old man any more than the kid wanted him. Less, probably...

"Gerald?" Roni prodded with a warning glance.

"What?" he all but snapped, glaring at her before glancing back at Pete with a disgruntled "Yeah, that's right."

Turning off the engine, Roni shot Gerald a look of exasperation, which he stoically endured before turning his back and stiffly getting out of the car. She glanced at the judge who gave her an encouraging smile.

"Time," he said, ushering Peter ahead of him out of the car. "That's what they need."

Gathering up keys and handbag, Roni sighed. "I know...."

Outside in the lot, Pete was immediately at her side and when she held out her hand, he grasped it like a lifeline.

"So." Inhaling deeply to conjure up enthusiasm, Roni cast a bright smile all around. "What'll we do first, shopping or carnival?"

"I vote for shopping," said the judge when everyone else just stood there shuffling their feet. "Let's see now, I need to get me some socks..."

"And Peter here needs a toothbrush, comb and things like that," Roni added.

"What're *you* after, Gerald?" Judge Cunningham said.

Not fatherhood, Gerald thought, still nursing his resentment. That was for damn sure.

His lips compressed, the look he sent Peter was moody. The little boy, catching it, quickly averted his eyes. Feeling like a heel, Gerald, too, glanced away only to find his gaze bouncing off Veronica's fierce and fiery green one.

Oh-oh, he thought. She's mad.

His chagrin intensifying, he quickly turned to the judge. "I, uh—" He cleared his throat. "I guess I need to get some..."

He really didn't need to get anything and wondered grimly why he'd even tagged along. His restless gaze was snagged again by Peter's apprehensive one. He felt a stab of regret that was almost painful and once again cleared his throat, but this time neither he nor the boy looked away.

"I guess I need to get some stuff for... for this new friend of mine to play with," Gerald said gruffly past a thickening lump at the back of his throat. Hesitantly, he reached out to tousle the boy's hair. "How about it, Pete? You like baseball?"

Peter only stared at him, silent and wary. But when Gerald leaned down, took his other hand and along with Roni began to lead him toward the mall, he didn't pull away.

Jauntily whistling, Judge Cunningham brought up the rear.

"Okay now, what next?" Roni asked after all their purchases had been made—and then some—and they were outside again in the parking lot. "Ice cream or rides?"

She smiled down into Pete's glowing face. "Petey, do you think you could part with that mitt and ball long enough to ride the merry-go-round, huh?"

Peter nodded, his smile shy. "I like the Ferris wheel," he confided.

"You *do?*" Roni, stowing the assortment of bags and boxes in the trunk of her car, acted suitably impressed. "Ever been on one before?"

Pete shook his head. "No, but—" he shot a glance at the judge " —I'm not a-scared of it."

"You're not, huh?" Roni laughed, tousling his hair. "Me, I've always been scared to death of that thing."

"You could come with me," said Peter with a hopeful inflection.

"I could? Hmm." Slamming the trunk lid closed, Roni considered. "I don't know..." She brightened. "Maybe if Judge Cunningham came, too...?"

"No, sir. No, thank you." Palms up, the judge backed away. "Count me out on this one!"

Roni had expected no less. She zeroed in on her real target, pinning him with a gaze that dared him to turn her down. "Or maybe Gerald...?"

She noted from the expression in his eyes that he condemned her to perdition, and with tongue firmly in cheek, told him, "I'm sure I'd really enjoy the ride if you came along."

She smiled her satisfaction when rueful humor and a glint of devilry lightened his gaze.

"Don't be too sure," he told her, but the scowl that had darkened his expression during most of their outing was replaced now by something a little easier. "I've always been pretty good at rocking the boat...."

"I'll just bet you have." There no longer was playfulness in Roni's tone. Instead, there was caring. "But that was *then,* wasn't it?"

"Come on, sonny," said the judge to little Pete, taking the boy by the hand. "Let's you'n me go buy some tickets."

"This is *now,* though," Roni continued when the old man and the child were out of earshot. "And there isn't just you to consider anymore."

In the pause that followed, their gazes lingered. Gerald wanted to argue, to say he owed no one but himself any consideration. That he hadn't asked to have fatherhood dumped on him, especially when the kid wasn't even his, and that going on joyrides at a hokey little carnival just wasn't his bag.

But those big green eyes holding his own wouldn't let him say those things. The goodness, the concern, the out-and-out forthrightness of Veronica's gaze dared him to be less good and less concerned than she was. There was a child here, it told him, a little boy who was innocent of any complicity, who was bewildered, lost and frightened. Father or no, Roni's gaze reminded, it behooved Gerald to make an effort.

With an inward sigh of capitulation—truth to tell, he'd gotten quite a kick out of the kid's pleasure over the glove and baseball—Gerald's lips twisted into a crooked, rueful grin.

"Yeah," he said, looking away from her to where the judge and Peter were standing in line at the ticket booth, Pete excitedly shifting from foot to foot. "I guess you're right. Now, there isn't just me anymore."

Surprisingly, knowing and admitting it felt pretty good.

"Line up to the right, folks," called the carny a few minutes later, herding Roni, Pete and Gerald ahead of him. "Up you go, missus—" He hoisted Roni into the swaying gondola, and Peter came next. "Scoot over, son," the man told him, "so your daddy'll fit, too. Watch your hands, everybody."

Safety bar in place, they ascended a few feet into the air, rocking gently as they waited for the one remaining gondola to be filled and the ride to begin.

Peter was craning his neck for a look at the judge who stood below them, grinning and waving and doing a thumbs-up. Gerald laid his arm along the back of the seat, resting his hand on Roni's shoulder as he did so and surprising her with a jolt of awareness.

He'd felt it, too, though. Warmth through the cotton of her shirt, a fragility of bone which, for an instant, translated itself into something almost electric that made his fingers twitch. He concentrated on the top of Pete's towhead, snugly nestled into the pit of his raised arm. Though Gerald knew the closeness was not by choice, it warmed him until his gaze fell on the little boy's hand, clutching Roni's slender one so tightly, the knuckles were white.

And he wished for a crazy second it were *him* Pete reached out to or that he, Gerald, might also have the comfort and reassurance of Veronica's hand.

He raised his head and caught Roni watching him. "Give it time," she said gently, just as the judge had earlier said to her, and unaware of any wish but Gerald's first one which the fleeting wistfulness of his expression had led her to surmise. "You're doing great."

Feeling foolishly self-conscious, Gerald shrugged with pretended indifference and looked away. Below, the world was a riot of color, the hurdy-gurdy carnival music a cheery accompaniment to the hustle and bustle of shoppers and merrymakers, while a potpourri of smells—popcorn, cotton candy, gasoline and more—almost, but not quite, overpowered the slightly floral scent Gerald had come to associate with Veronica Sykes.

Funny, he mused, his head tilting back now as he gazed into the cloudless, endless canopy above their heads and deeply inhaled. When he wasn't looking at Roni, only sensed her, smelled her, thought of her, he always perceived her as beautiful. But when he looked at her...

He tilted his head and gazed at her face. In profile, her strong nose, no-nonsense mouth and stubborn chin was defined against the azure sky like a scissor-cut cameo, clean and precise. She had many fine features, he noted, not the least of which was an abundance of shiny dark hair that fluttered like a banner in the breeze. Silky little tendrils of it were caressing her cheek and getting caught in the corner of her mouth....

Impulsively Gerald lifted his hand and pushed them away. And with his fingertips gently brushing lips that felt sleek as warmed satin, with cheeks kissed by the sun and pinked with excitement, and with her meadow-green eyes swinging to his, startled and aware, Gerald was surprised to discover once again that Veronica Sykes wasn't nearly as plain as first impression might lead one to believe.

It was Thursday, five days later. Taking his customary extra hour for lunch for his visit with Frank Tillman, the parole officer, Gerald was striding down the street toward the federal building. He felt pretty good, even though he'd made no progress in getting information out of the boy regarding his nana's whereabouts. He felt he'd made progress otherwise, though. Pete seemed less afraid of him and, well, he was less afraid of Pete.

Matter of fact, when the boy had awakened, crying, last night, Gerald had felt confident enough to handle the crisis on his own. Instead of getting in a panic and hustling Roni out of bed, he'd simply scooped up the boy into his arms and taken him into his own bed with him.

Pete hadn't struggled, though he'd lain there stiff as an overstarched sheet for a bit until Gerald had started to talk. Quietly with his arms folded behind his head and eyes closed, he'd begun to tell the boy how as a kid he used to be scared in the night now and then, too. No shame in that, he'd told Pete. And no shame in missing his nana.

And, boy, had he been surprised when Pete had come out and said, "I don't miss Nana with Roni here. Mostly I just miss Arf."

"Arf?"

"He's my dog, and Joe doesn't like him, and—"

"Who the he—the *heck* is Joe?"

"Nana's boyfriend. He kicks Arf."

"Sounds like a winner," Gerald had said with dry distaste, raising up on an elbow to peer down at the boy who now lay trustingly curved toward him.

"Nuh-uh, he isn't," Pete had countered solemnly, reminding Gerald that kids tended to take things pretty much at face value. "He's a good-for-nuthin' drunk, Nana says."

A fine place to leave your son, Marcy Kemp! Maybe "Nana" was smart to bring him to me....

The boy had eventually gone to sleep nestled against Gerald's back, and he'd still been there that morning, when Gerald had snuck from the bed to go to work.

"How's everything going?" the parole officer now asked, flipping through Gerald's file with an air of pre-occupation. "Job okay?"

"It's fine."

"Still not interested in finding something better? Seems a waste—"

"Maybe so," Gerald interrupted. He didn't want to get into a long discourse about his cowardice—for that's

ACCIDENTAL DAD   85

what it was and he knew it—when it came to looking for a better job. "But for now I'm okay with what I'm doing. I've still got a lot of adjusting to do."

"Such as?"

"Well, I've got this kid living with me now...."

"Oh?"

Something in Tillman's tone made Gerald's antennae rise. "Any problem with that?"

Tillman frowned. "What kind of kid?"

"A boy." Gerald fidgeted, a sense of unease making him wary. Tillman's attitude had changed from semi-interested to sharply interrogative.

"Yours?"

"That's what it says on the birth certificate."

"But...?"

Gerald didn't even bother to think before he answered, knowing Pete's fate would be sealed if he showed any kind of doubt. "But nothing," he said, shrugging. "The kid's mine."

"Mother?"

"Dead."

"I see."

Cold-blooded bastard.

But Gerald didn't realize *how* cold-blooded, until the following Monday when Tillman called him at the boardinghouse. It wasn't a long conversation, and when it was over, Gerald looked grim.

"What is it?" Roni asked worriedly, not liking the careful way with which Gerald avoided her searching gaze as he slowly replaced the phone nor the jumping muscle in his cheek. It was the only thing in his face that moved, and that worried her, too. "Bad news?"

He looked at her then. "A couple weeks ago I would've said no." Crossing his arms, he turned to stare out the window.

"But now?"

He laughed without humor, just a short bark. "Now I'm so mad I could—" Swearing, he spun around to face her. "They want Pete!"

Roni reared back. "Who?"

"The man, that's who. The au-thor-i-ties!" He enunciated each syllable of the word with bitter distaste. "They've decided an unmarried ex-con doesn't make for good parenting material."

"B-but..." Roni gripped her head, trying to understand. "How do they...? I mean, who even told them...?"

"Me, dammit, that's who." Slamming a fist into the palm of his other hand, Gerald paced. "I told my parole officer."

"Well," Roni said, trying to calm her own rising dread—she'd grown to love little Pete; how could she let them take him?—as much as Gerald's visible agitation. "I mean, why wouldn't you tell him, right? After all, the man's supposed to help—"

"Why wouldn't I tell him?" Gerald demanded furiously, planting himself in front of her with such menace, Roni knew a fleeting urge to cower she wasn't about to give in to. "Me of all people? I'll tell you why I shouldn't have told him—because I should've known better, that's why! Didn't those same authorities jerk me around all my life? Didn't they stick me here, stick me there, always thinking they know best when what they know is diddly-squat!"

Breathing hard, he said nothing more for a while, and only stared at her. The bleakness of his expression was almost more than Roni could bear.

"Gerald..."

But he shook his head, rubbing a hand across his face and looking away. "The only place I was ever happy at, the only home I ever knew, they yanked me out of after just three months because somehow they found out the couple I was living with wasn't married. They were in their forties and they'd been together for eighteen years. The guy's wife was in a mental institution, incurably insane, but he didn't want to divorce her. That's how good and decent he was."

Gerald closed his eyes against the pain he'd buried so deep, so long ago, he'd believed it gone. Yet here it was, as fresh and as wrenching now as it had been then. "But according to the *authorities,*" he said heavily, "this man was not good and decent enough to be a father to a dumb little orphan like me...."

Roni felt Gerald's pain as keenly as if it were her own. She touched his arm, and when he opened his eyes to look at her, tried for a smile, which wouldn't quite materialize.

"It's what you want, though, isn't it?" she said quietly, forcing herself to play devil's advocate and thereby hopefully make Gerald see. "To have the boy taken off your hands..."

Gerald stared at her as if she'd lost her mind. "But not like this," he said fiercely. "Not by *them!* I mean, I've been there, lady. And I'd sooner keep the kid with me forever—"

"Is there a chance that they'd let you?" Roni interrupted with a glimmer of hope kindling in her eyes. "Is there anything *I* can do, do you think?"

"Do? *You?*" Raking a hand through his hair, Gerald looked up at the ceiling with a harsh, self-mocking laugh. "Oh, sure," he drawled sarcastically. "Let's see now—"

He pinned her with a gaze that was as blue and cold as glacier ice. "You wanna get married?"

Chapter Six

"Get married?" Flabbergasted, Roni reared back. "To you?"

"No, to Santa Claus," Gerald wisecracked sarcastically, stung by Veronica's reaction to his impulsive and admittedly unorthodox proposal. He hadn't really been serious, but did she have to act as if it were the most lunatic idea she'd ever heard? "Of *course*, to me," he said with a scowl. "You did say you wanted to help, didn't you? Well..."

Shrugging, he let her draw her own conclusions and moodily turned to stare out the window.

Veronica, her heart racing, glared at his back. To be married to Gerald Marsden. To be able to touch that splendid body, to be held...

"That's not very funny." She was appalled that her first reaction had been to say yes to his throwaway proposal when, obviously, Gerald had only been using her as an object on which to vent his frustration. "In fact," she added, miffed, "I can't believe you'd even joke at a time like this. "

"Neither can I," Gerald said dryly from his post at the window, and confounded Veronica—and himself—a second time by flippantly adding, "But then, maybe I wasn't joking."

After which, without bothering to await Roni's reaction, he pivoted on his heel and stalked out of the room.

So what was *that* supposed to mean? Thoroughly rattled, Roni stared at the closed panel. Had the man gone crazy?

It had to be the heat, she decided, starting to pace and putting a not-quite-steady hand to her own perspiring brow. Everybody went a little nuts when the mercury shot up into the high nineties.

Marry Gerald Marsden?

Her head began to pound right along with her heart. He hadn't been serious. In spite of that baffling rejoinder with which he had left her, surely he hadn't been serious.

Had he?

At a loss, Roni let her hand drop to her side and told herself it didn't matter whether he'd been serious or not, because there was no way she'd ever be willing to marry Gerald Marsden in any case. Even if he *was* the most gorgeous man she'd ever beheld, and sort of endearing, to boot. There was just no way. Except...

Roni paced to the window and stared out of it, seeing nothing. Next door, Rufus began to bark, meaning Marge Benson was either going out somewhere or returning. Accustomed to the never varying procedure, Roni didn't spare the racket more than half an ear and none of her mind. The latter was asking her, *What about Peter?*

There was the rub, wasn't there?

Tilting back her head, Roni drew a ragged breath. If by marrying Gerald she could keep the little boy she'd come to love, then shouldn't she do it?

Oh boy! Another long breath was tremblingly released. To help Peter, to keep him from uncaring strangers, to give him love and a home—could there be a better cause for her to become involved in? And… To marry Gerald, to maybe have the chance to give him a sense of family and belonging he'd never known before. Wouldn't that be a worthy challenge?

Oh boy, oh boy! Roni wrapped her arms around herself to ward off the shiver of nerves and of—yes, of anticipation—that rippled across her skin and raised goose bumps. She could do some real good here, she told herself, *if* Gerald were really serious about them getting married, and *if* that really would be the way to keep Pete out of the authorities' clutches.

It wouldn't hurt to check into it, now would it?

"I'd like to see Mr. Tillman, please," Roni said to the tired-looking woman behind the paper-littered desk.

The woman didn't look up. "You got an appointment?"

"No, I don't. I called earlier, but—"

"You a new parolee?"

"No, I'm not. I—"

"What's this about?"

"Look—" Roni possessed many admirable qualities, but patience with bureaucracy was not one of them. Besides which she was not about to discuss her personal business with someone who had yet to look her in the face. "Is Mr. Tillman in or isn't he? I know he was out when I telephoned earlier but I was told—"

"He's in."

"Well, thank you." It took an effort not to sound sarcastic. "Do you suppose I could speak with him?"

At last the woman snapped shut the file she'd been making notations in and raised her eyes. There were bags of weariness beneath them and her mascara had smeared. Everything about her face shouted that it had been a long day. Considering the nature of this partic- ular government office's business, Roni could believe it.

"I'm Veronica Sykes," she said, her tone warming. "If you'll please tell me which room and if Mr. Till- man is free..."

"He's in 305." The woman's long-suffering attitude didn't change in response to Roni's little olive branch, but she did add, "Second door on your right."

"Thank you."

A moment later, Roni was in Tillman's office and, once again, introducing herself.

"I'll only take a moment of your time, Mr. Till- man," she added, taking the seat Gerald's parole offi- cer had politely indicated. "It's in regard to Gerald Marsden."

Tillman, leaning back in his chair with lips pursed against steepled forefingers, wordlessly nodded for her to go on.

Made a little nervous by the man's cool reserve but determined not to show it, Roni looked him in the eye. "I, uh, I'm Gerald's...fiancée." She only stumbled very slightly over the falsehood. "We're going to be m- married very shortly."

"Really?" Coming alive to the extent of sharply arching his brows, which gave him a slightly sinister appearance, Tillman studied her with interest.

His keen regard, given her precarious hold on the truth, raised Roni's inner quaking by several points on the Richter scale.

"Funny," Tillman mused after a while in which Veronica was hard-put not to fidget. "You'd think Marsden would have mentioned it. Is this a fairly recent development?"

"R-recent?" Roni's voice cracked and, growing annoyed with herself, she sharply cleared her throat, stiffened her backbone and reminded herself that she was doing nothing *bad* here, for Pete's sake. Quite the contrary.

Right.

Her chin came up. "If you want to call two years recent...."

"Two years?" Fully alive now, Tillman straightened in his chair with a who-are-you-kidding kind of look on his face. "It seems to me that two years ago your *fiancé* was in prison clear across the country, while—if I'm not mistaken—you, Miss Sykes, were residing right here in Salem, Oregon, and operating...what's it called?

He flipped his Rolodex to "Marsden" and read aloud, "'Roni's Boardinghouse,'" before turning his flinty gaze back on her. "Now isn't that true, Miss Sykes?"

"Quite true, Mr. Tillman." Challenged like this and knowing her cause to be honorable, all of Roni's civil militancy as well as her dignified schoolteacher persona rose to the fore. She drew herself still more fully erect and never batted an eye. "Gerald and I met through the mail. We corresponded for three years before he proposed.''

"Pen pals, eh?"

"At first, yes, that's what we were. In time, however, we..." Roni sternly forbade herself to blush beneath Tillman's slight sneer "... we fell in love and—"

The need to clear her throat would no longer be denied as she thought, *If Gerald heard this, he'd have fits.* She coughed delicately into her fist and, summoning every ounce of poise she possessed, briskly added, "In any case, we're planning to marry and have Gerald's son, Peter, live with us. Just as he is already doing."

"I see," the parole officer drawled with heavy emphasis.

"Which brings me to my actual reason for coming to see you today."

"Now why doesn't that surprise me?" A glimmer of genuine humor made Tillman's face seem much more human.

Roni took heart. Maybe the man wasn't the ogre she'd cast him to be in her mind. Maybe he didn't really lie awake nights devising ways of wrenching little children out of loving homes.

She leaned forward entreatingly. "I'm a schoolteacher by training, Mr. Tillman," she said. "I love children, and I love little Peter. Gerald Marsden has paid his debt to society. He is a good man and he—" She swallowed, nervous again. "He wants to do right by the boy...."

Which was certainly true.

Tillman's gaze remained thoughtful, but after a moment he slowly nodded and said, "I'm sure that's true, Miss Sykes. And please believe me when I tell you that the state wants first and foremost to do what is best for the child. In most cases, that means keeping him or her in the care of the natural parents whenever possible. . . ."

Later, back in the boardinghouse, Roni still couldn't believe how pleasantly the interview had ended. Almost giddy with relief at having the matter resolved, she was anxious to get Gerald in private, bring him up-to-date and present him with her offer to marry him for Pete's sake. She wouldn't be able to, however, until dinner and Peter's bedtime bath were out of the way.

What the hell did he know about bathing a kid? Gerald groused moodily, his steps dragging on their way upstairs. Nothing, that's what. And what was more, he hadn't had any plans of ever learning. So how had he gotten himself roped into doing the job tonight? One of the others would have been perfectly happy to do it, just as they had been ever since Pete had landed on their doorstep.

"He's *your* son," Roni had said, ignoring Gerald's automatic "He's not," as if he hadn't said a word. "The last couple of days you've been so aloof with him again and it hurts the little guy. You've got to start reaching out more, Gerald, or he'll never start feeling close to you."

"He's scared o' me."

"Well, honestly—can you blame him? Half the time you look ready to bite a chunk out of his hide and the other half you ignore him."

"That's because I'm scared of him, too." He had surprised himself with the admission, but, apparently, not Veronica.

"I know," she'd said, her censorious expression—her schoolmarm face, as Gerald privately called it—softening into one of empathy. "But you're the grown-up here...."

"Says you," he'd tossed in so glumly, it had made her laugh.

"Go on," she'd urged gently, giving him a little shove. "Go up there before he shrivels into a prune. He's been in that tub for half an hour now, playing. And, Gerald...?"

"What?"

She'd turned uncharacteristically shy, making Gerald wonder what was up, and if it had anything to do with that loony exchange they'd had the previous evening.

"Could I talk to you later?"

"Sure."

Fine. Later. This was now, however, and here he was, upstairs, and with zero idea of what to do next.

Carefully, hesitantly, Gerald pushed open the bathroom door, but didn't move beyond the threshold right away. Instead, unnoticed by the little boy making engine noises as he propelled a plastic soap dish through the water, he stood and silently observed the child at play.

With Peter's back toward him, Gerald was free to let his gaze roam the slight body and take stock. Lord, but the kid was skinny. Along his curved spine, every vertebra stuck out like bony knuckles on a fisted hand, and with nothing but skin covering it, his rib cage resembled a washboard. Hunched over as he was, his shoulder blades protruded like pointy little angel wings....

He was so little. And so defenseless sitting there naked in that tub.

Unbidden, emotion painfully tightened Gerald's chest. It wasn't the first time the sight of the boy had called forth this kind of reaction, but it was neither welcome nor comfortable. Almost angrily, he fought to toss it off.

"Playtime's over," he announced, stepping all the way into the room and sounding much sterner than had been his intention. Seeing the boy start and jerk his head around to show a frightened face, he inwardly swore and could have bitten his tongue.

"Water must be getting cold," he said, forcing his tone and expression to lighten up. He hunkered down and stuck a finger into the water. "Brrrr . . ."

The hoped-for smile didn't materialize. Peter continued to regard him warily. "Leo said he'd come'n wash me," he said after a bit.

"Well, I'm here to do it, instead." With his finger, Gerald gave the floating soap dish a little shove. "So what kinda boat have we got here, huh? A cabin cruiser or something?"

Pete shrugged, abashed, and ducked his head. "I's just pretendin'. . . ."

He awkwardly gathered up the dish, nailbrush and three plastic spoons that had served as his fleet and put them on the rim of the tub, leaving Gerald feeling inadequate and clumsy.

"So, uh," he said, his eyes on the cowlick that made the hairs at the crown of Pete's averted head stand on end, "how're we gonna do this, huh? Shampoo first— is that how it works?" He picked up a bottle and studied it. "This the stuff to use?"

Since he was perfectly able to read the label, the question was merely a ploy to get the boy to relax and talk to him. It seemed to work; at least to the degree that Pete turned to quizzically regard him.

"The others already know all that stuff," he said. "How come you don't?"

Relieved to have breached the boy's defenses once again, Gerald gave him a wry half grin. "I guess it's because I've never given a kid a bath before."

Pete digested that, all the while earnestly studying Gerald's face, but no longer looking scared.

"How come?" he asked after a moment during which Gerald did his best to look nonthreatening and at ease. The latter of which he definitely wasn't.

"I guess because I never had a chance to," he said, meeting Peter's wide-eyed gaze as levelly as he could. "I never, uh, had a kid before, y' see."

Another moment of mutual silence and measure-taking ensued. And then Pete said, "I never had a dad before, neither." And after a couple of heartbeats, added, "Nana said..." But then his courage seemed to desert him.

Loath to lose what little ground he'd just gained, Gerald encouraged, "What did your nana say, Pete? Tell me."

"She said..." Faltering, the little boy visibly swallowed and the eyes he slowly returned to Gerald's face suddenly brimmed with tears. "She said she was...was gonna take me to live w-with my...m-my d-dad, but..."

His lower lip pitifully quivered and two big tears crested the dam of his lower lids to roll in twin rivulets down freckled cheeks.

"But..." Gerald prompted, not far from having his own lip tremble, and wondering with a kind of helpless and undirected rage why being a kid had to be so damn tough. And he asked himself how he could make it easier on this one. At least for a little while.

Start reaching out more. Roni's voice. Inside his head, but as clearly audible as if she were there in the room with him.

"But y-you, you're n-not..." Though Pete was crying in earnest now and couldn't make the words come out, Gerald didn't need to hear them to know what they were.

You're not my dad.

Damn right, he wasn't, Gerald thought grimly, but somehow didn't find any satisfaction in reiterating that. On the contrary, he caught himself wishing he really *were* the father so that he could put an end to the kid's misery.

The latter seemed crucial suddenly. Pete's choked little sobs were breaking his heart. Clumsily, he rubbed the boy's bony back and tried for a note of exaggerated outrage. "Who says I'm not?"

Evasions, he figured, were not outright lies and, in this case, infinitely kinder than a statement of truth.

The sobs hiccuped to a stop. "N-no-b-body..."

"Well, then, what the hel—heck?" Cupping Peter's wobbling chin, Gerald urged his face around. "What're you talkin' about then, huh?"

"I jist..." Pete shrugged, his eyes round and hopeful now as they clung to Gerald's face. "Y-you never s-said I could c-call you D-Dad."

"I didn't? Well, shoot—" Somehow, Gerald managed a crooked smile as he playfully touched a fist to Peter's bony shoulder. "I figured you'd know to call me that all by yourself, but I guess that was pretty dumb of me, huh? Tell you what..."

Picking up the washcloth, he tenderly began to wipe Peter's face. "Let's make a deal, okay? From now on, if there's anything you're not sure about, or if something bothers you, you come and talk to me right away, and we'll do our best to work it out man-to-man. How's that?"

"F-fine," Pete mumbled, and emerged from behind the washcloth with a smile so bright, Gerald was nearly blinded.

About an hour later, Leo Kominsky and the judge were doing battle on the chessboard in the parlor. Louise and old Miz Henks were doing needlepoint and discussing the bedtime story that had been read to Peter that night. Reading to the boy had become an established ritual which the old librarian took very seriously and eagerly looked forward to. Somehow, Pete had managed to sneak past her defenses and into her heart just as he'd done with the others.

Roni was lounging in the porch swing, her long legs up on the seat, her feet tucked beneath her. One hand was holding her hair off her neck, the other was languidly fanning her face with a dog-eared paperback. She was wondering how best to broach the subject that was on her mind, but could think of no delicate way.

And so all she said was "God, it's hot."

"Yeah." Gerald stood at the porch rail, one hand resting against a porch post, the other buried in the pocket of a baggy pair of shorts. Though he'd replied to Roni's remark, he hadn't really heard it. He was deep in troubled thought and had been ever since he'd finished tucking Peter into his cot.

He had never been emotionally close to anyone and had never wanted to be. Closeness scared the hell out of him, as a matter of fact. After that fiasco with the only foster parents he'd let himself grow to...like, and who had genuinely liked him in return—they had already applied for his adoption when he'd been taken away from them—he had never allowed anyone to get close to him again. Not even Marcy, who'd been helpless most of the time, as well as harmless and sweet and a friend. But even her he hadn't allowed into that part of him that had once been so hurt.

And he wasn't about to let anybody into that part now, either, he grimly vowed. Though Pete was getting close. Damn close. Too close.

And that was scary, since there was no chance he could—would—keep the boy. He had a life of his own to build. He had years and years of living to catch up on and, damn it, authorities or no, just as soon as the grandmother had been tracked down—and she would be if it was the last thing he did—the kid was out of his life.

And you're gonna miss him like crazy.

With a weary sigh, Gerald let his forehead drop against the pillar. How, he asked himself, had his life gotten so complicated again so fast? Here he'd thought that once he was out of prison it'd be a cinch to keep things simple. Eat, sleep, work. Keep to yourself, keep your nose clean and mind your own business. That's the advice Big Mike the lifer had given him and that's how he'd planned things to be—simple.

Except nothing had been simple ever since he'd come to this burg. He who'd always been a loner now had people coming at him from all directions. Worse, they were people he liked, cared about, didn't want to hurt. Who needed that stuff? Hell, he was still adjusting to freedom, to normalcy—whatever *that* was—to life as a regular working stiff.

Straightening, he lightly pounded a fist against the pillar and thought, So why couldn't he simply let the authorities take the boy now, before Pete got any closer, and before he—Gerald—ended up getting hurt again?

Gerald knew the answer even as he stared unseeingly at the ugly purple house across the street in front of which a skimpily clad couple had stopped beneath the street lamp to kiss. The reason he couldn't was that—to him—it would be the ultimate cruelty and, no matter what else he was and might have been, cruelty had never been part of his makeup.

So where did that leave him? Fighting a system he'd fought all his life without winning even once, that's where. And there was no way he could beat them now, either. Unless . . .

He raised his head and slowly turned it toward Roni only to realize she'd been looking at him all along. Through the gathering gloom of summer evening dusk, their gazes connected and Gerald thought, Unless he gave some thought to that marriage thing.

"Mind if I join you on that swing?" he asked.

Roni wordlessly tucked her legs closer and patted the spot next to her. She suspected that her pose and lazily fanning hand motions were probably making her seem completely relaxed and at ease but, in truth, she was one big knot of nerves.

Gerald sat down beside her with both feet squarely on the floor, but he draped his right arm along the back of the seat much the way he had done on the Ferris wheel. He didn't look at Veronica, but the combination of body heat and floral scent that emanated from her like a physical touch had him very much aware of her proximity. He kept his eyes straight ahead to where an assortment of shells strung along various lengths of fishing line hung from an overhead beam. They twirled, chiming musically, in the barely stirring breeze.

"So how'd the bath go?" Roni tossed down the paperback and folded her arms, hugging herself to contain a sudden shiver of awareness and anticipation. In a moment she'd bring up her visit with Tillman.

Gerald gave a dry little laugh, not looking at her. "I hardly flooded the bathroom at all."

"I'm glad to hear it." Roni chuckled, too. "But that's not what I meant."

"I know." He shot her a fractured grin. "Don't worry, I did plenty of reaching out. Everything's hunky-dory."

"That's good." *Now, Veronica.* "Um . . . The reason I wanted to talk to you . . ."

"Yeah?"

"I, uh, I went to see your Mr. Tillman today."

"Say what!"

As if stuck in the rear by a cattle prod, Gerald shot off the swing and Roni visibly started. She had expected Gerald to be a little taken aback maybe, but never had she imagined him to react with such wild-eyed outrage.

"How dare you?" he charged, all but breathing fire.

And in response, her own tightly wound nerves snapped. She, too, leapt to her feet. "If it means keeping that little boy here with us," she informed him through tightly clenched teeth, "then, mister, I dare anything."

"Tillman's *my* business."

"Not when it comes to Pete," she denied hotly. "You've made that boy my business, too."

"All right, all right." With both palms up, Gerald let out a long breath and pulled himself together. "I'm sorry."

Roni nodded, almost but not quite, mollified. "After you brought up that marriage thing last night—"

"No!" Shocked again, Gerald stared at her aghast. "Say you didn't tell him about that."

"I told him about that."

"Oh, man." Groaning, Gerald covered his eyes.

"Not only that, I told him we were engaged."

"God, please let me only be having a nightmare...."

Pretending calm, Roni continued as if he hadn't spoken. "The deal is, if you and I get married, Pete can stay."

"Terrific. Just swell." Gerald kept his face buried, thinking, *If we get married*... and felt as if a noose were being tightened around his neck.

"Dammit, Veronica..." He lowered his hand and met her gaze with an expression of anguish. "I wasn't really serious about that last night."

"Weren't you? Well—" Roni resolutely told herself she'd known all along he hadn't been. "Considering what's at stake here, I thought it worthwhile to investigate the possibilities."

"The possibilities..." Gerald shook his head, frowning at her. "Are you telling me you'd be willing to do this thing, for Pete's sake?"

Roni shrugged, trying hard to sound nonchalant. "For Pete's sake, maybe I would. Wouldn't you?"

"Sweet Mother Murphy." Staring into her calm face, Gerald thought he knew now what the guys on death row must be feeling as the final day of reckoning approached. Terror, pure and simple. "Sure, I'm willing to do what I can," he said after a bit, squirming. "But *marriage . . . !*"

A short and very crass expletive followed.

Roni's ears burned. "It was your idea," she primly pointed out, turning her back on Gerald and his agony. "I was only trying to find out the facts of the matter since that is the only way to make intelligent decisions."

"Marriage," Gerald said again from in back of her, but weakly now. "Sweet Mother Murphy . . ."

Jamming his hands into the back pockets of his shorts, he went to stand at the railing again and tipped back his head to stare at the sky. "That's heavy stuff, Veronica."

"I know." Suddenly exhausted, Roni plopped back down on the swing but didn't set it in motion.

"It's so damn—" Gerald shrugged helplessly.

"Binding," Roni supplied.

"Yeah." There sure were a lot of stars up there. "It sounds so—"

"Final." Why was he going on about it? What was he thinking?

"Uh-huh." A bit unsteadily, Gerald sucked in air. "It's a really big step. . . ."

"Huge." It was almost as if... Roni straightened out of her slump. "It's scary."

"No kidding." A heavy silence followed. Gerald was still staring up at the sky, breathing hard, while Roni hardly dared to breathe at all and was staring at him.

"Any idea how long it'd have to be for?" he finally asked.

Roni shrugged, and struggled to swallow that tight and hurting thing in her throat. "For how long will you be on parole?"

"Three years, give or take a couple months."

"Well, then . . ." Another shrug Gerald didn't turn around to see. "It'd have to be for three years, or at least until we've got Peter's grandma tracked down."

"Pshhh . . ." Another harsh release of air from Gerald.

"By the way, are you working on that?" Roni fervently wished he'd say no.

Gerald said yes. He was, sort of. "I talked to a P.I. a couple of days ago and he told me he'd get right on it. Not that we have a heck of a lot to go on. California's a big state and there's no place called Bisto on the map."

Thank goodness, Roni thought, but aloud all she said was, "That's true." She was tired now and . . . Well, she was tired.

Gerald studied his hands, unable to deny that marriage did indeed seem to be the only way to hang on to Peter even as he called himself an idiot for ever having brought that particular notion up in the first place. Marriage. Damn, it was a drastic step.

"Three years," he mused with a grimace, the prospect of three whole years of marriage causing him almost physical pain. He might as well be back in prison. And, married to Veronica Sykes, what the *hell* would he do about . . .

He shot Roni a quick and speculative glance.

. . . sex?

She wouldn't expect him to be . . . faithful, would she? Unless, of course, whatever agreement they came to on this included—

His gaze snapped back down to his hands. It wouldn't. Of course, it wouldn't. So what the hell was he supposed to do about—

"Three years *is* a long time," Roni conceded.

"Sure is." *An eternity when you don't have your freedom and can't have sex.*

"A lot of things can happen."

"Yeah." Gerald's short laugh was part snort. "People could really grow to hate each other in three years."

"Or," Roni said, giving release to a renewed attack of anxiety with a nervous little laugh of her own, "just as bad, they could do just the opposite and fall in love."

There followed a silence so complete, a falling snowflake would have sundered it with the force of a sonic boom. Very slowly Gerald turned to face Veronica and they contemplated each other without speaking for what seemed like a very long time. Roni was waiting for Gerald to say something. Gerald was wondering what to say.

Should he ask her? Should he do this crazy thing and ask her?

Would he ask her? Should she do this crazy thing and tell him yes, if he did?

He didn't ask. He stood staring at her for what seemed like an eternity and still he didn't ask the question.

Her throat tight with a wealth of emotions she couldn't begin to name, but which certainly included the bitterest of self-recriminations for having brought them to this awkward and embarrassing pass, Roni stiffly got up off the swing and walked into the house.

Chapter Seven

The following Thursday was the Fourth of July and though it had been fairly easy for Veronica to avoid being alone with Gerald Marsden for the past two days, the boardinghouse's traditional picnic and outing was likely to put an end to that.

Roni hadn't wanted to be alone with Gerald after that evening on the porch. She was embarrassed, she was hurt, she was disappointed and, yes dammit, she was angry!

So, all right, maybe she was no prize by cheerleader / beauty queen standards—she had no illusions about that. She knew she was too tall and thin, too pale of skin for the vividness of her dark hair and eye color, and had a nose that might have looked patrician on a man, but on her merely dominated.

She wasn't pretty. Those men who liked her—and there were quite a few—liked her as a person and friend.

She just wasn't the type to inspire the males of the species to write sonnets or become crazed by lust. So be it.

At one time she might have wished it were otherwise, but she had long since come to accept the status quo with the kind of resignation that sprang from the belief—taught by her aunt and uncle—that there was nothing but misery to be gained from fretting about the unchangeable. She had plenty of good things going for her—intelligence, health, compassion for others—and she had enough self-esteem to know she was not unlovable!

Matter of fact, she told herself self-righteously, she was a lot more lovable than Mr. Gerald Marsden who was much too good-looking, much too moody and not a heck of a lot of fun to be with most of the time.

To think she'd been willing, out of the goodness of her heart, to go along with a harebrained idea that had been *his* in the first place. Hadn't he said maybe he *wasn't* joking? And then not even to ask her!

It was too much. Whatever else she might not have, she did have pride. And she would not be the one to bring up that subject—or any other—again.

But... And this made her so mad she could weep. What about Pete?

The last thing Gerald had envisioned himself doing on the Fourth of July was to spend the day at some fool picnic with a quartet of septuagenarians, a woman in a snit and a five-year-old kid who daily wormed his way more deeply beneath his skin.

Independence, he groused as, at the crack of dawn on this holiday, he was carting the third cooler of food and drink out to the van and balancing it on top of the pile of lawn chairs, umbrellas and portable barbecue already there. Independence might be what the day was all about for everybody else, but other than that month in Lauderdale after his release from prison, *he* hadn't had any more independence on the outside than he'd had in.

Dammit, would there never come a time when he could do what *he* wanted to do and that's all?

Mount Hood Meadows—what the hell would he find there besides horseflies, ticks and stinkweed?

"The best dang fishing hole this side o' the mountain," Leo proclaimed, stowing two fishing poles—"One for the boy"—his tackle box and net.

"A kid can only play so much catch and listen to so many fairy-tale stories," he added. "I, my good friend, aim to teach your son the manly art of fishing today."

"You do that," Gerald muttered sourly. *Your son.* "Me, I plan to take a good, long siesta just as soon as we get there."

"Young people," scoffed Judge Cunningham, coming down the porch steps with a watermelon tucked under each arm. "They eat vitamins by the handful, exercise by the hour and still they got no stamina. Why, when I was your age, Jerry m'boy—"

"Judge!" called Louise from the house, thus once more earning Gerald's gratitude. "Did you put the charcoal in the van?"

"Sure did, Lou!"

"Good." She turned to holler into the house for Roni, then came briskly down the front walk and climbed into the van. "I say let's get this show on the road."

In spite of himself and his earlier announcement, Gerald had way too much fun to ever take his planned siesta, though now that everyone had devoured huge quantities of barbecued hamburgers, hot dogs and corn, it seemed he was the only one who wasn't sleepy.

Pete had curled up on the blanket between Judge Cunningham and Leo Kominsky, tuckered out from a morning of untangling fishing line from tree branches and the like, while Louise and Miz Henks reposed with hands folded across their matronly midsections on a couple of poison-green webbed lounges.

The only ones awake were Gerald and Veronica.

Though where Roni was at this moment was anybody's guess. After the meal she had rather curtly announced she was going for a walk and marched herself down along the path that took off to the right from their picnic spot.

Maybe he'd stretch his legs a bit, too, Gerald thought, rousing himself from the lawn chair in which he'd been lazing while his food settled. Except he'd take that other trail leading into the bush from the opposite side of their clearing.

This place really was something special though, he mentally conceded a short time later as he meandered along the winding path and inhaled the woodsy tang of conifers and brush, of wildflowers, musty earth and ripe vegetation none of which he knew by name.

Until now, he hadn't known what he'd been missing stuck as he'd been in the city's asphalt jungle and, later, in that concrete mausoleum of a penitentiary. There was a whole other world out here, a world too many kids like he had been would never get a chance to explore.

Fishing... It had been really something, watching Pete and old Leo up to their knees in that stream, casting out the line, reeling it in, talking and laughing companionably. A man and a boy, enjoying each other and the day.

I should've been the one out there with Pete.

The thought arrived unbidden along with a retroactively forlorn feeling that he'd once again been left on the outside looking in.

And I should be the one he should be napping with, too....

Manfully forcing those petty grudges aside—he could hardly justify being resentful when, more often than not, he was the one holding back—Gerald forced a reminiscent chuckle, recalling how often Pete and Leo's lines had been caught up in some branches instead of being down in the water.

Pete sure had been excited though when Leo had actually managed to hook a small trout. Whooping and hollering, he'd rushed up to Gerald, grabbed his hand and, almost tripping over himself in his eagerness, had made him come look at the undersize fish before it was let go.

How good that little hand had felt in his....

Remembering, Gerald experienced again that warm, heart-expanding rush of affection the touch of Peter's hand had caused. At that particular moment he'd wanted nothing so much as to be able to pick the boy up and hold him close to his heart.

And promise him he'd always be safe and happy.

He couldn't do that, of course. About all he *could* promise, ever, was that he'd make damn sure the state wouldn't take this kid and steal his childhood from him.

And the only way to do that, Moose m'boy, is to ask Veronica Sykes the question you should've been man enough to ask her the other night.

Pensive, awed by the majesty and splendor that surrounded him, Gerald slowly turned in a circle, admiring the stately pines and firs, drinking in the clear, clean air and thinking that no way would he allow anyone to rob little Peter of . . . all this. Matter of fact—

He stopped the thought, waiting for the proverbial second thought to follow up and negate what he'd been about to think. When none came this time, he thought, So that's that.

It seemed like he was going to have to find Veronica right now and get this thing resolved.

Gerald didn't have far to look. Roni was perched on an outcropping of rock at the edge of the same stream Pete and Leo had fished in. The path Gerald had chosen to set out on turned out to be part of one big circle. At about the halfway mark from the picnic spot was where he came upon her.

She hadn't heard him approach and he stood for a bit and looked at her. She sat with her arms loosely wrapped around her long, slim, drawn-up legs which, next to her emerald eyes, Gerald considered Roni's best feature. Her chin was propped on her knees; little tendrils of hair had escaped from the braid at the back of her head and gently fanned ear and temple on the side of her face.

As before, the reality of her plainness was somehow at odds with the mental image of Veronica he'd formed. And the gracefully dreamy picture she made up on that rock made her seem like the mythical Lorelei, singing a siren's song to unwary sailors, come to life.

The crazy thing was, just as those mariners had been unable to resist the call of Lorelei, so Gerald felt himself drawn to the woman up there on that rock. Drawn by some undefinable attraction, nudged forward as if by an invisible hand.

"Roni," he called quietly, when he was only about three feet away and still she had not moved. He didn't want to startle her—the steady rush of water over the boulders in the stream made a sound that mimicked and amplified the sway and rustle of wind-stirred leaves overhead, and she had not heard his approach. He wanted to honor her privacy, should she wish it, and not intrude uninvited.

At his call she turned her head so that only her cheek still rested on her knees. She didn't seem overly surprised to see him and studied him soberly for several long moments before she said, "Come on up if you want."

"I find it restful here," she added, when he'd settled himself next to her. She straightened, supporting herself with both hands propped behind her and looking straight ahead over the frothy stream and beyond to wooded hills and puffs of white cotton clouds. "Peaceful."

Following the direction of her gaze, Gerald nodded. "This is a whole new world for me, you know."

"I guess it would be." Roni closed her eyes, savoring the moment, feeling Gerald next to her although they weren't touching, and savoring that, too. "It never gets old, either."

"Veronica..."

"Hmm?" She kept her eyes closed.

"I made you mad the other night—"

"Why don't we just forget it?"

"No." He touched her arm and when she opened her eyes and looked at him, said, "I hurt you in some way. I should have said something—I wanted to—but I..."

Compressing his lips into a thin line of self-disapproval, he shrugged and lamely added, "I guess I froze up."

"It's all right."

"No, dammit," he said heatedly. "It's not all right. You haven't talked to me since, for crying out loud."

Roni pulled a face, chagrined, but decided to be honest. Surely, being adults, they could be honest. "To tell you the truth, I've been feeling too...uncomfortable and, well, foolish to talk to you."

"Foolish?" He frowned his consternation. If anyone had been acting like a damn fool about Pete, it'd been him "Why, for Pete's sake?"

Roni quietly laughed. "You just said it there, didn't you? For Pete's sake." And, when his frown deepened, she elaborated by saying, "*Marriage* for Pete's sake, is what I mean. I felt that by bringing the subject up to you the other night, and by having gone to Tillman to investigate all the ins and outs, I'd made you feel as if I was putting pressure on you. As if it was *me* you had to marry—"

There, she'd said it. Searching Gerald's face for clues to his thoughts, she looked so vulnerable, he was quick to tell her, "Roni, don't you know that you're the only woman I'd even consider marrying?"

"No..."

Gerald scowled. "Well, you are."

Something unfolded inside Roni's breast, something that had been hurtful and tight, but which blossomed now, even as she cringed at Gerald's choice of words when he went on to say, "I mean, who else is there? Aside from the fact that I don't know any other women, Pete's crazy about you. And any fool can see how you feel about him...."

Gerald knew he was blowing this but couldn't seem to find a way to state things with more feeling and diplomacy.

"Not to mention," he said, "that you already told Tillman—"

"All right, all right." Having decided that gallows humor was the only means by which to salvage even a shred of her pride, Roni held up her hands in a gesture of mock surrender. "Enough of this sweet talk. Go ahead and pop the darn question and put us both out of our misery."

With the wind thus taken out of his sails, Gerald momentarily floundered. It occurred to him that, whatever else being married to Veronica Sykes might or might not turn out to be, it wasn't likely he'd ever be bored. And, thinking that, he almost felt better.

He cleared a throat that had suddenly constricted and turned to her. Roni was gazing at him levelly, her face grave.

His was, too, as he looked her in the eye and said, "Veronica, will you marry me?"

He saw her swallow, saw her lashes flutter, and—this he felt as much as saw—a flash of pain in her eyes as she nodded and softly said, "Yes," before quickly averting her gaze.

He had hurt her again. Gerald didn't know how, and he didn't fully understand why, but intuitively he knew that this was at least as much, but probably quite a bit more, painful and difficult for Roni than it was for him.

What a bastard he was, he thought with patent self-disgust. Bellyaching to her about having to get married and losing his freedom and garbage like that when it was she, Veronica, who was really making the sacrifices here. She'd never known Marcy and could feel none of the mixed emotions he was feeling toward that woman—affection, pity, regret, and resentment for sticking him with her kid. The only thing motivating Veronica was compassion. Out of compassion she was willing to give three years of her life to an ex-con and his problems. How many women would make such a gift to a man?

Not many.

But this one had, and she deserved for him to make this moment special.

Hesitantly—for all her generosity and friendliness with others, Roni tended to be skittish around him at times—Gerald took Veronica's hand and cradled it in both of his. "Roni, could you please look at me?"

Reluctantly she did.

"I want you to know I really appreciate what you're doing," Gerald told her. "You won't be sorry...."

But as Roni gazed into the intensity of his blue eyes and goose bumps chased hot flashes up and down her back, she thought, Oh, God, I'm already sorry. And more scared than I've ever been in my life.

"We'll do this strictly by your rules," Gerald was saying. "I won't touch you—"

"You're touching me now," Roni said, and opened her eyes. "I've got no problem with that." The understatement of her life. She *loved* the feel of his hands around hers. They were so warm, his hands, so big. The callused hardness of his palms was so reassuring somehow. These hands could cope...

"I meant..." Uncomfortable, searching for a tactful way to put this, Gerald blew out a hiss of air and let go of her hands. "You know... Intimately, is what I meant."

It hadn't been all that long since he'd had a woman, yet suddenly he craved one as if it had been years. Roni's sleek and endlessly long legs were suddenly very much on his mind, and awareness of the full swell of the breast that was only an inch or two from his side made Gerald's palms itch and his mouth go dry with wanting. "Unless you...?"

The unfinished question quivered between them like an arrow in its target. Somehow it became impossible for either of them to speak or look away. As if a force field had been created around them, currents of energy flashed palpably between their bodies and tinglingly tugged them toward each other.

Roni's breast was no longer a mere titillation of the mind, it was a very real, very warm and infinitely arousing caress against Gerald's upper arm. Her eyes, wide, aware, brilliantly green, were only an inch or so from his unblinking ones. Her breath, sweet and clean, was his.

And then her mouth was, too.

A groan—his? hers?—was swallowed in a kiss that went instantly beyond merely friendly. Open-mouthed, hot and needy, this was a first kiss like no other Gerald had ever experienced. Nor was the heat, the need all his. On the contrary. It poured from Roni in a response so powerful it made him shake. She came to rest against him, supple and yielding, inch for inch. Those miles of legs he'd admired were entwined with his, satin to grip. Her arms were soft and fragrant bands of steel around his neck, holding him to her as he was holding her to him. Close, but not close enough.

Never had he kissed like this. Never had he *been* kissed like this! With utter abandon, with no holding back. With passion that was every bit as generous, as wholesome and as honest as was the woman from whom it flowed.

"Veronica..." Things were moving too fast. He was burning up. In another minute any further discussion of the kind of marriage theirs was to be would be moot, and though he'd like nothing better right now than to let nature take its course, this was hardly the time or the place. Nor was Roni likely to thank him for it later.

Relaxing his embrace was almost beyond him. It took more effort, concentration and sheer force of will than anything he'd ever done. Pulling his lips from hers was physical torture. Seeking to lessen the ache of it, he nuzzled the velvety skin of her cheek, her neck, the hollow of her throat. "Roni..."

"Hmm?" She caressed his cheeks, smoothed an eyebrow, traced the proud sweep of his nose, then looked into the blaze of his eyes and took fire again. Gripping the sides of his head, she pulled his mouth to hers. And once again they were lost.

Everything inside Roni was alive. Her blood raced through her veins, propelled by a heart that was a wild thing in her chest. Heat was everywhere. Need was all-consuming. Caution was a thing she might never have known. And yet, suddenly it was there, like a fireman with a hose, dousing the flames. Cooling the heat.

And though the fires still smoldered, she drew away to once again look into Gerald's eyes. Questioning. Not what they'd shared, but what lay ahead. Needing answers, reassurance. Perhaps seeking immunity from the inevitable hurt she knew lay in store for her further up the path they—their bodies, their passion—had chosen to take.

But instead of the answers she sought, all she saw in the shimmering blue that rivaled the sky was a reflection of everything she was feeling, and one thing more. Regret.

Chapter Eight

Everything that happened after Gerald's fateful proposal of marriage up on the rock above the stream, seemed to happen with the speed of a film stuck in fast forward.

Predictably, Aunt Louise and the boarders were delighted that their matchmaking efforts had paid off so swiftly and completely. They squabbled for days over who had done the most to bring the desired result about, with Aunt Louise taking the bulk of the credit, which all the others privately disputed.

Peter had nothing much to say initially. It took him a couple of days to adjust to this latest upheaval in a status quo he had barely begun to be comfortable with. Gerald and Roni gave him time to mull over and digest things before each of them took the boy on a little outing in the course of which they explained to him that nothing would essentially be changing. He'd continue to live at the boardinghouse; he wouldn't be leaving the doting "grandparents" the boarders had become to him.

Roni and Gerald did some talking, too. What with the wedding date set for the first of August—only a few weeks away—and what with Gerald agreeing that it made perfect sense for them to keep living in the boardinghouse, Roni had decided that Aunt Louise in particular, but the others, too, had a right to know about his past. All of it. Gerald, old reflexes being as difficult to change as old habits, had panicked at first, but eventually agreed. As Veronica had predicted, the boarders—having come to love and respect Gerald— listened gravely and afterward, individually, had expressed their approval and support.

Judge Cunningham, always the unappointed, but nevertheless well-respected, spokesman of the group, had summed up their feelings this way: "I knew from the start you were a troubled man with a troubled past, Jerry m'boy. But I also knew—and I've seen 'em all— that you were one of those who're basically *o-kay*."

He couldn't have given Gerald—or Veronica, for that matter—a finer wedding gift and blessing.

As to the wedding itself, no fuss, no frills was the deal. This distressed Aunt Louise who'd had visions of Veronica as a radiant bride all in white, and of herself in a light blue mother-of-the-bride concoction complete with hat. Economics rather than lack of sentiment were given by Roni as the reason for keeping the affair as low-key and simple as possible. And, being a realist, Louise could do nothing but concur this would be best.

She would not hear, however, of the betrothed couple's intended sleeping arrangements. In fact, she was scandalized and lost no time telling Roni so in the course of one of their nocturnal heart-to-hearts.

Roni was in her customary spot at the foot of Louise's bed. The wedding was only two weeks away and this was the first opportunity the two women had had since the "engagement" to have a talk. Or so Veronica said. Truth was, she had been purposely evading her aunt's veiled invitations until now.

With her fingers worrying the quilt, as they were prone to do when she was thinking or, in this case, stalling, she wondered how best to reply to Louise's offer to give up this master bedroom to the newlyweds. Including the king-size bed she used to share with her dear George, and which only last year had gotten a brand-new mattress.

One option would be for Veronica to be perfectly candid and say, "Aunt Lou, Gerald is only marrying me for Pete's sake, and sleeping together is not part of the deal."

Yeah, right. And break her aunt's heart. After all, Louise considered herself the matchmaker here and fully expected to see the couple *she* had brought together to live happily ever after in the fullest sense.

Another option, of course, would be to merely say, "Thanks, Aunt Lou. We really appreciate it," take possession of the bedroom and let nature take it's course.

That option held quite a bit of appeal, given the fact that Roni found Gerald anything but repulsive and, after that fiery engagement kiss they'd shared, the idea of more of the same and beyond never failed to make her pulse rate go off the chart.

If only she were sure that Gerald's pulse was pulling similar stunts. . . .

But she wasn't. In fact, quite the opposite. She clearly remembered the look of regret in Gerald's eyes after their kiss. The look had said he wished he hadn't done it as clearly as if he'd spoken aloud. And he certainly had done nothing even remotely like kissing her ever since. Not that Roni had made any overtures, either. It seemed neither of them was sure of what the other expected, and circumstances being what they were, talking to each other at the level of intimacy required for such a talk—well, obviously neither of them was ready for that. And so, the only time they touched these days was by accident, such as when they handed each other something that had to be passed at the table.

Oh, they were cordial to each other—after all, pretending to the boarders and Aunt Louise that they were merely feeling reticent about hugging and smooching in front of them only went so far in the credibility department. They *had* to be nice to each other, even fondly smile at each other, and they did.

They also did things together with Pete, things such as getting him on a Parks Department T-ball team and going to his practices and games. Or they'd take him swimming at nearby Washington Park pool, where Gerald generally ended up being ogled and drooled over by every female over the age of twelve.

For his part, Pete hardly seemed to be the same shy, sullen little tyke who'd arrived at their doorstep a scant six weeks before. He acted like any normal little boy with two doting parents and some other reinforcement—the boarders—in reserve: increasingly cocky and outgoing, endearingly affectionate and bright.

At the pool with Gerald and Pete, unaware that she was the only female able to stir up Gerald's hormones, Roni did plenty of discreet ogling and salivating herself. That man—Gerald—had *some* body, she noted as her juices flowed. Wow! But even so, turned on as she'd be at those times, to her the most attractive thing about Gerald was that he seemed totally without vanity, and courteous enough to pretend to be oblivious to all women other than herself.

He really was a very nice man, she admitted dreamily. And the idea of sharing a bedroom—come on, Roni, you mean a *bed*—daily gained in appeal. Unfortunately, one person's lust did not an affair make! Or a proper marriage, either.

Which, confronted by Louise's expectations, left Roni with option number three. Evasion.

She now raised her head to let her eyes meet her aunt's, and got a shock. Somehow lately, Louise had aged. She looked every one of her seventy-three years and more. Without her glasses on, her eyes were the faded, myopic, somewhat rheumy eyes of the old, and it seemed to Roni that a whole new network of wrinkles had established themselves in her aunt's face. When?

Her gaze sharpened. "Are you all right, Aunt Lou?"

"Don't change the subject," Louise said crossly. "We're discussing bedrooms here and for the life o' me I don't know what you're thinking so long and hard about."

"Well, I'll tell you." Roni was not so easily put off. "Just as soon as you answer my question first."

"I'm fine."

"You look tired."

"Of *course* I look tired," Lou snapped, "it's near midnight, for heaven's sake. Now. What's with the bedroom?"

"Well…" Fidgeting, Roni thought, Gosh, but I wish I was better at lying. "Actually, Gerald and I had thought to… you know, leave the sleeping arrangements as they are for the time b—"

"What!" Louise sat bolt upright, her face like thunder. "And whose harebrained idea was *that,* as if I didn't know?" Leaning forward, she shook a finger at her niece. "Now you listen to me, missy. Being shy with a man is one thing—"

"I am not shy with men, Aunt Louise!" The idea!

"Sure you're not." Louise snorted contemptuously. "That's why we've had such hordes of 'em beatin' down our doors all these years."

"I hate it when you get sarcastic, Aunt Lou."

"And I hate it when you get prissy, so we're even." Lou's voice and demeanor abruptly softened. "Listen to me, pussycat, a man like Gerald Marsden doesn't come down the pike every day o' the week—"

Amen to that, Roni thought. And wasn't it a good thing, too, for who could survive such a thing?

"And they don't go around asking a woman like you to marry them, either. For whatever reason," she added when Roni would have interrupted with a heated, What do you mean, a woman like me?

Her aunt's little codicil to that inflammatory statement shocked her into silence, however. A silence during which the two women somberly gazed at each other, and the increasing length and weight of which was measured and disturbed by only the ticking of Aunt Lou's old-fashioned bedside clock.

It was Veronica who finally broke it by asking, a bit defensively, "Just what're you saying, Aunt Lou?"

The old woman's face seemed to become more drawn, her eyes more tired. She closed them a moment and took a deep breath.

"I'm sayin' I know darn good'n well that there's stuff goin' on with Gerald that the two o' you don't want me and the others to know about. And that's fine. People are entitled to their privacy, I always say, and I'm not generally the kind of person who'd stick her nose where it didn't belong. Except when it comes to me and mine, and who else have I got but you?"

She opened her eyes to fix them on Roni who had drawn breath to speak, when Louise stopped her. "There's more I want to say, and I want you to pay attention 'cause it's important. Things aren't what they should be between you and Gerald and I'm sure there's a good reason. I may be old but I'm no dummy, and I figure the two o' you have your reasons for doin' this thing. It's Pete, I figure, and I got no problem with that. What I do have a problem with, is how you, my girl, are so dad-blamed willin' to throw away the chance of finding true happiness with this man—"

"Aunt Lou—"

"I asked you not to interrupt, Veronica."

"But you don't understand...."

"And haven't I just said so a minute ago?" Louise snapped. "What *you* don't understand, Veronica Sykes, is that whatever the reason for you'n Gerald getting hitched, you got a chance here to make it work. Think, girl! And for once be a little selfish."

Selfish?

"You gotta be feeling something for the man to be willing to marry him, Roni."

Roni fidgeted uneasily, not saying yeah or nay. Not even saying it to herself.

But Louise didn't need the words. Her gaze shrewd, she reached out and patted her niece's hand. "I say go for all of it while you got the chance. . . ." Sinking back into her pillows, yawning, she muttered, "And don't you dare say, 'all of what?'"

Roni was weary. On top of all the tearing up of herself she'd been doing these past few days, she didn't need more of the same from her aunt. Besides . . . "It takes two to tango, Aunt Louise."

"Very true, pussycat." Louise yawned again and snuggled deeper. "But you get them two people on the same dance floor and play the right tune, and you can bet it won't take but minutes before they'll be doin' the fanciest tango and then some."

In spite of her weariness, Roni had to laugh. "Honestly, Aunt Lou. . . ."

"Well . . ." Louise chuckled, too, but only briefly. Quite serious again, she said, "All I'm sayin', hon, is nobody ever caught a fish without baitin' the hook and droppin' it in the stream. You're a wonderful, lovable person, Veronica Sykes, and Gerald Marsden would have to be a fool not to know it. All you gotta do is give the man time and opportunity to admit it, to himself and to you. If you really want him, that is."

Did she really want him! If only things were as straightforward as that. "There's more to this than merely me wanting the man, Aunt Louise. Gerald has many things to resolve—"

"So who better to help him resolve them than you?"

"There's still a lot about him you don't know, Aunt Louise. . . ."

"I understand that. But as long as *you* know, what's it matter?"

"He's been hurt. . . ."

"I know it," Lou said sadly. And in response to Roni's quick, questioning glance, she added, "You're not the only one in this family who cares about the underdog, pussycat. I knew he'd seen his share o' pain and trouble the minute I first clapped eyes on the man. My heart went out to him, right then and there. And I took him in...."

For a moment, the women smiled at each other with genuine affection. "You're a deep one, Louise Upshot," Roni said after a bit. "And a crafty old she-devil, too."

"So you'll take the bedroom?"

Chuckling and helplessly shaking her head—the woman had a one-track mind!—Roni climbed out of bed and went to kiss her aunt good-night.

Upstairs in his room, meanwhile, Gerald lay tense and awake in his bed. Arms crossed beneath his head, he stared into the murky darkness, listening to Peter's deep breathing and asking himself for the umpteenth time how in the hell he'd come to this pass?

Here he was, a guy who, as short a time as six months ago, could only dream of parole and life on the outside, now pretty well saddled with a wife and family! Sweet Mother Murphy, how had it happened?

Hadn't he all his life been a loner? Hadn't he all his adult life sworn to stay that way? To be accountable to, and responsible for, nobody but himself? Did he have any idea what he had let himself in for here...even if it *was* supposed to be only temporary?

Hell, yes, he did! And it was scaring him out of his wits. Which were exactly what he must have lost to have gotten himself trapped into this situation in the first place.

Make that *talked* into, instead of "trapped," he amended grimly, restlessly letting his cocked leg straighten and plop down on the mattress. That damn woman had talked him into this whole infernal fiasco, and that included keeping the boy until the grandma was found. He would never have kept the kid without her looking at him with those sparky eyes of hers and moaning about what a poor little tyke Pete was.

And then to go over his head to Tillman, telling falsehoods he'd have had a hell of a time trying to disclaim or get out of and sulking around afterward, making *him* feel guilty! Who needed it?

Who needed a kid clinging to his knees, grinning up at him with Marcy Kemp's soulful eyes and worming his way into a man's heart?

Marcy! Thoroughly disgusted, Gerald jerked his one leg up again and let the other one plop down on the bed. She'd been another prize example of wily womanhood.

Weren't they all like that, women? Weren't even Louise and old Miz Henks putting the squeeze on him in their own sweet way with their wedding plans and talks of romance and stuff? Yes.

And, in the end, there was always good old Mom, wasn't there?

Without her doing what she'd done— Couldn't you at least have given me a father, *Mom?*—his whole life would have been different. None of this would have gone down.

Little Peter and Veronica Sykes would've been nothing and nobody to him.

So what're they to you now, Moose?

Unable to stay lying down any longer, or even in the room, Gerald surged up off the bed, stepped into his jeans and headed out the door. Tip-toeing down the stairs, avoiding the by-now-familiar ones that creaked, he made his way to the front door. He eased it open and stepped out onto the shadowed front porch. The dim street lamp at the corner across the street was scant illumination; it only served to deepen the darkness hugging the corners and recesses of the porch.

The cool night air caressed Gerald's bare torso like a lover's hand. He breathed of it deeply—freshly cut grass and car exhaust—and began to feel a little easier. Wishing he still smoked, he went to stand at the railing and stared out at the purple house on the other side, its color now mercifully neutralized by the night.

It came to him that he'd stood just like this the night Veronica had confessed to having gone to see Tillman. She'd been on the swing over there, with her long legs bare and her T-shirt clinging to heat-dampened skin. He'd gotten a hint then of the treasures she kept hidden beneath the loose shirts and blouses she was prone to wearing, but at the swimming pool with Pete he'd since been getting quite an eyeful on a regular basis.

This lady was built! Skinny where she ought to be skinny, she was anything but everywhere else.

It had been a revelation to Gerald, Veronica's body, and if the woman had been any other than the one she was, he might have been tickled to death. Given the kind of relationship they were launching into, however—marital sex, or any other, for that matter, had not been discussed and wasn't likely to be—he'd gotten to be one very frustrated and miserable man, thanks to some ten days and nights of increasingly vivid fantasies that left him sleepless and aching....

He might have gone to find someone with whom to relieve that ache, but every time he'd even come close to actually dressing up and heading out, an image of Veronica Sykes and her damn green eyes would show up to ruin the mood.

Aw, hell . . .

Bone-tired, thoroughly confused and not a little scared, Gerald let his forehead drop onto the hand resting against one of the porch pillars.

In two short weeks he'd be a married man, and then what?

"Gerald?"

He heard her say his name at the same time he heard the creak of the swing. Sweet Mother Murphy, she was out here! And then he felt her touch on his skin, and whirled around.

She backed up a step, her eyes in the semidarkness wide, luminous, mysterious.

"What're you doing out here?" he demanded, ready to bite her head off because she'd caught him with his guard down and . . . hurting.

"It's my porch," said Veronica, arms crossed in front of her and chin out. She was not about to be snapped at when she'd only wanted to . . . what? Reassure him or something. "I can come out here anytime I damn well want."

Because she never swore except in the mildest way, Gerald's brows shot up in surprise and amusement tugged one downturned corner of his mouth in the opposite direction. "Sassy tonight, aren't you?"

"Yeah, well . . ." Roni found herself grinning, too. "I get that way around belligerent he-man types."

"He-man types, huh?" Imitating her folded-arm stance, Gerald leaned his rump against the railing and regarded her. His fiancée. He let his gaze travel over her and abruptly dropped his arms and stood straight. All she had on was a man's undershirt. The tank-top variety. With no bra, no—

"Hell," he swore, tearing his eyes away and looking up at the ceiling. "Don't you even have any underpants on?"

"I beg your pardon?" Roni didn't think she'd heard right. What kind of thing was that for a man to say to his landlady? All right, his fiancée.

"How can you come out here in the middle of the night practically naked?" he demanded in a furious whisper, keeping his eyes carefully on her face. "Don't you know there's perverts running loose just waiting for someone like you to—"

"Oh, for crying out loud!" Roni erupted. "Listen to you! You'd think I was parading down Broadway, New York, instead of standing on my own private porch in little ol' Salem, Oregon! Besides which, I do *so* have panties on. See?"

And up came the shirt to expose French-cut bikini pants, as well as the tiny waist and slender torso which, Gerald knew all too well, farther up supported the sweetest pair of—

"For crying out loud, Veronica." He raked a hand through his hair. His voice wasn't working right. "Pull that shirt down, will you please?"

She was already doing so, her moment of temper having been replaced by chagrin the instant she'd gotten a look at Gerald's expression. "I'm sorry...."

"Yeah." He turned to look out at the street again and audibly inhaled. "Me, too."

Roni backed up a step. "I think I'll go to bed now...."

"Okay. G'night."

"Gerald...?"

"What?"

"Aunt Lou wants us to have her bedroom after we're married."

Halfway through the sentence, Gerald had begun to turn around, and now he was staring at her again. He couldn't think of a thing to say— God, he wanted that more than anything—and searched Roni's face for a clue to *her* feelings knowing his immediate response was hormone induced and, consequently, enthusiastically in favor of Louise's idea. All he could make out on Veronica's countenance, however, was anxiety-edged nonchalance.

And a white-knuckled grip on her own upper arms.

She was nervous. And, one glance into her wide, shimmering eyes convinced him, somehow...expectant, too.

The realization nudged him forward, toward her. About a foot away, he reached out to lightly skim the palms of his hands over her upper arms in the barest of caresses.

The ragged catch in her breath and a slight shiver were Roni's only reaction to Gerald's touch, but it was all the encouragement Gerald needed to gently tug her unresisting body closer.

"Roni..." His hand slid around to her back, down past the curve of her waist to where his fingertips barely touched the pleasing swell of her buttocks, and back up again along the curve of her spine. His head lowered, his cheek touched hers, and then his lips were nuzzling where his cheek had been.

"Roni," he said again in that same husky whisper as his mouth moved moist and warm across her skin. "What is it *you* want, sweetheart?"

Oh, Lord. Squeezing her eyes shut, still hugging herself inside Gerald's embrace and feeling a tremble creep up from her toes and through her body, Roni wondered if a person could faint from the kind of excitement and hunger that was gripping her.

What did *she* want?

What a question. With Gerald's lips on her neck, his naked chest an inch from hers and his hips even less than that, with his arms around her and his fingers making spine-tingling forays through the generous armholes of her shirt—what did *she* want?

Him.

She straightened her fingers and unfolded her arms to wind them tightly around his middle and thus close the small gap between their bodies.

She wanted him.

She turned her face and caught his lips, opened her mouth and welcomed his tongue.

She wanted him. She felt him move, spread his legs, pull her closer, his hand now racing across her back, now cupping her, cradling her—and knew with giddy delight that he wanted her, too.

The moment Roni's mouth had searched out his, Gerald was lost. Wild for her, he took what she offered, taking care to give back what he took in equal measure and to pleasure her as she was pleasuring him.

Touch, tug, fondle, stroke. Clasp, hold, feel... Their hands were busy. Their lips were insatiable.

Just as the first time, Gerald and Roni seemed incapable of holding back. They kissed endlessly, deeply, erotically. They kissed as if the union of their mouths were the ultimate joining and nothing more was needed to make them one.

Needs were fulfilled, new ones were born and, their tongues entwined and rhythmically stroking, those needs, too, were met.

Almost. Almost.

With a deep-throated growl, panting, Gerald tore his mouth from Roni's at last and dropped to his knees in front of her. Groaning, he wrapped his arms around her and buried his face against the flat of her belly.

Roni felt this strong man tremble and, flooded with tenderness, cradled his head and stroked his hair. They were breathing hard, both slick with perspiration and increasingly, regretfully aware, as their immediate passion receded, that this would be as far as things could possibly go between them this night.

"You won't be sorry," Gerald whispered against Roni's damp shirt, bunched beneath his cheek at her midsection. "We'll be good together, you and me. For as long as it lasts...."

For as long as it lasts.

Roni's fingers stilled in his hair. The shiver racing down her spine was chilling now. Her heart stopped beating for a moment, and started up again at a much more subdued pace.

Of *course* only for as long as it lasts, she was telling herself. What did you expect without love?

Sensing the change in her—she seemed to have gone still all over—Gerald lifted his head to look up at her face. As he did, Roni's hands fell to her sides.

"Veronica? Sweetheart, what is it?" Releasing her, he got to his feet as Roni backed up a few steps. "Did I hurt you? Did I say something?"

"No." Roni's smile took an effort but no way did she want Gerald to know what she was feeling just then. He was only being honest with her, after all, by stating things as they really were, not as she suddenly wished them to be. He was pulling no punches, spared no thought for sweet words and romance.

And why should he? He wasn't the one throwing the monkey wrench into the works. *She* was.

He wasn't the one who had fallen in love.

Chapter Nine

Although the next several days had an unreal quality and were pretty much a blur of activity, Veronica's heart and mind were only on Gerald, and very much in conflict.

She had done a stupid thing—she had fallen in love with the man who was marrying her only as a matter of convenience.

Her mind thought that this was not only a hoot, it told Veronica that it was the ultimate in stupidity and just the sort of thing a professional bleeding heart like herself would do.

Don't just agree to help the man out, Ron old girl, her mind jeered. Don't just give him a month, a year or even two or three years of your life, give him your heart, too, why don't you?

Her heart. Ever tender, it urged her to go ahead and love him. He deserves to be loved, it would say. He *needs* to be loved. And in time, it whispered on a note of bittersweet longing, maybe, just maybe, he will learn to love you back.

Oh, sure, Veronica, her mind heckled. The day hell freezes over.

He's a man who's been abandoned, unloved, all of his life, her heart rationalized. First by a father who didn't care enough to stick around and see his child born. Then by his mother, for whatever reasons—and surely they had been desperate ones. And then by a society too bogged down by red tape and bureaucracy to concern itself with individuals until those individuals, floundering, ran afoul of the same laws outside of which they'd been forced by an accident of birth and circumstance to exist.

It's time he knew he counted with someone, her heart said. Me. Gerald Marsden counts with me.

And, watching him toss balls to Pete, or mow the boardinghouse lawn, or play checkers with the judge and chess with Leo, or flirt with Lou and Miz Henks while laboring with hammer and nail up in the attic, Roni would amend that declaration to include all those people.

He counts with *us*, she would say to herself. With Pete and me and all the others.

And when her mind jeered, Yeah, but for how long will you have him to care about? she used Gerald's words to shut it up. For however long it lasts.

Which maybe, just maybe, could be a very long time. Meanwhile, she wouldn't fret, she would not borrow trouble, but she *would* do everything in her power to be a helpmate and a wife, and a mother to Pete. And maybe, just maybe, make Gerald love her in return.

August the first. His wedding day.

More at odds with himself than ever—he'd vacillated between panic and nervous anticipation at least hourly since asking Roni to do this thing with him— Gerald knotted his tie for the third time in ten minutes and swore roundly at fingers that were clumsy with nerves. He glared at his image in the mirror and swore some more, until the appearance of another face in the glass next to his abruptly shut him up.

"Having trouble with that tie?" Roni was determined to be happy and optimistic on this important day.

Gerald was too scared and nervous to be likewise disposed. "Get out of this bathroom."

"Listen," Roni said, summoning all the cheer and bravado she could while battling long-dormant feelings of inferiority at the splendidly handsome sight Gerald made in the mirror next to her. His good looks made her own face seem all the more homely to her. "I clean it, I get to be in it whenever I want."

"Testy, aren't we?" Humor overrode nerves for a moment, and Gerald grinned at her. "But you forgot to say, 'damn well' this time," he added, referring to that other night when she'd gotten her back up. Roni's presence never failed to improve his mood these days, and was all it took to remind him that this was a good thing he was about to do.

And didn't she look good enough to eat today, too, and smelling like the meadow full of flowers they'd walked through on the Fourth of July? Chuckling as she was at his little dig, she was actually pretty.

"Yes, well," she was saying, "that's because you seem to be doing enough swearing for the both of us these days." Her large eyes turned serious. "Cold feet at the eleventh hour?"

Gerald didn't beat around the bush. "And at the second, fifth and eighth hour, too."

"It's not too late to change your mind, you know."

"That goes for you, too, Veronica."

She shook her head. "That's not how I am."

"Well..." Gerald's sigh came from deep inside of him. "I guess, that's not how I want to be, either, for once." Frowning, he went back to fumbling with his tie.

"Want me to do that for you?" Roni asked.

"No, I got it." He turned away from the mirror. "What do you know about knotting ties, anyway?"

"Plenty." Roni hung up a towel Gerald had used and leaned on the side of the sink, secretly savoring the implied intimacy of the small task. In just a few hours, she would be officially entitled to perform little wifely chores such as these all the time. Her heart sped up at the thought. "Uncle George used to have me do his every Sunday before church."

"He must've been something, your uncle." After taking the jacket of his brand-new suit off the peg on the back of the door, Gerald shrugged into it. "You and your aunt are always talking about him."

"He was quite a guy."

"Quite a carpenter, too, judging by the way this house was put together, and by those tools of his Louise dug out."

"Tools that *you,* Mr. *Architect,* put to remarkably good use building that bedroom for Pete in the attic."

Resolutely willing the surge of love and pride for this man from showing in her eyes, Roni reached up to smooth Gerald's lapels. "What other secrets are you keeping, hmm?"

With his gaze held by Roni's, and seeing all manner of unfathomable emotions lurking there, Gerald tensed with sexual awareness. Sex, having Roni naked and willing in his arms, had been very much on his mind this past little while. Slowly, deliberately, he let his gaze drop to her lips. They were invitingly full and soft, and parted expectantly beneath the gathering heat of his gaze.

"I guess," he said, his voice growing husky, "the fact that I want you *is* no secret, huh?"

"No." Closing her eyes a moment as her throat did the same, Roni shook her head. "It isn't."

"Tonight," Gerald growled, hauling Roni against him for a punishing kiss that instantly gentled as she melted into him. "Tonight there won't be anymore holding back, will there, Veronica?"

"No." With a tremulous smile, Roni touched his cheek. "No more."

A little over an hour later, the deed had been done. The proverbial knot had been tied and, surprisingly, it didn't feel as much like the knot of a noose as Gerald had feared it would.

"Son," said the justice of the peace to Peter, who was looking spiffy in a much smaller version of Gerald's pin-striped suit, "you may now kiss your mother and dad."

Grinning shyly—the first time he'd been shy in many a week—Peter edged toward Roni who dropped down on one knee before him and gathered him close.

"C'mere," she murmured, glorying in the feel of the little body in her arms and raising shining eyes to Gerald who stood solemnly watching. Behind him, Aunt Lou and Mrs. Henks dabbed at moist eyes, while Judge Cunningham noisily harrumphed and Leo trumpeted into his handkerchief.

Keeping Peter in her arms, lifting him as she straightened, Roni moved with him over to Gerald. She held out a hand to him and, when he'd clasped it in his, drew him closer. Peter half turned in her arm, encircling Gerald's neck with his own free one, and so they stood close for long moments in a three-way hug.

Family.

The word exploded into Gerald's mind and heart like a bomb. *His* family. For as long as it lasted, he'd be a loner no more.

They'd had a catered champagne supper at the swank old Carlton Hotel. Aside from the boarders, a few of their pals from the Senior Center had been invited to come celebrate the happy occasion. They'd all long since adopted Pete as their own grandkid-in-residence and had followed the developments at the boarding-house with the same fervor they brought to their daily dose of *All My Children* on TV. With their own lives' endings all too near, the happy endings of other people were what they hung in there for, rooting. They had a grand old time at the wedding.

Roni's friend Sarah—a soulmate in causes of every description and herself as yet uncommitted to any one man—had been there to throw rice at the happy couple, as had the burly foreman from Gerald's job in construction. Big Mike had sent a telegram of congrat-ulations from Munson Island that read, "Atta boy, Moose. Now get out and be a *man*. Get a *real* job!"

After the celebration meal, Pete and the old folks had climbed into the van that the Senior Center had gra-ciously provided and headed back to the boarding-house.

Sarah and the foreman, both flushed and looking smitten, left together, arms entwined.

Gerald and Veronica, on the other hand, had taken the elevator up to the bridal suite, a night in which had been Aunt Louise's wedding present.

They stood just inside the door to the sumptuous room in the middle of which stood the largest darn bed

Roni had ever beheld, and which she found impossible to ignore. Still, nervous and tongue-tied with each other in a way they'd never been since the first day they'd met, Roni and Gerald both did their best to pretend not to see it as they moved farther into the room. They were each carrying a small bag of overnight necessities and made projects out of setting them down on opposite ends of the couch that was part of a sitting arrangement fronting the fireplace at the far end of the huge room.

Making the occasional, appropriate oohs and aahs, they meandered around to admire this and that, all their attention ostensibly centered on knickknacks and decor when in actuality they were excruciatingly aware only of each other.

And that bed.

"Ah!" Gerald exclaimed, the relief in his voice at having found something worthy of vocal expression mirroring the look on Roni's face as she swung away from the window she'd been pretending to look out of, and faced him.

"Champagne." Squinting, he read aloud the small card that was propped against the ice bucket. "Congratulations and best wishes to Mr. and, uh—" Here he faltered, his voice roughening so that he had to clear his throat in order to go on. "—Mr. and *Mrs.* Gerald Marsden, from the management and staff of the Carlton Hotel."

He glanced at Roni and forced a smile. "Pretty decent of them, isn't it?"

Roni felt as if her lips were stuck to her teeth, it was so hard to stretch and curve them in a smile of response. "Sure is."

"'Course—" He made a sound that could almost, but not quite, pass for a chuckle, while thinking with a horrified sort of incredulity, Why the hell are we having this asinine conversation? "—at the rates they charge..."

"Really." Roni's chuckle was counterfeit, too. Her fingers were twisting into a pretzel the ends of the tie-belt that was of the same pink patterned silk as the very flattering, swirly skirted dress she had on.

Gerald, whose gaze had gotten lost in Roni's, blindly reached for the bottle, hoisting it as he asked, "Think you could handle another glass?"

They'd had a couple at the supper, but he sure as hell needed something to get him past this blasted awkwardness. Dammit, what was it with him, anyway? He'd had plenty of women in his time and not even the very first one had had him this uptight.

"Sure," Roni said, dismally wondering if all newlyweds were this uncomfortable and awkward, or was it just them? The way Gerald was looking at her, so hungrily. So...

Something hot and alive shifted low in her belly, and her mouth went drier still as she choked out, "Why not?"

It took an effort for Gerald to break their charged and prolonged eye contact long enough to fiddle with foil and twisted wire, and to get the plastic cork to pop. It finally did so with satisfying force, allowing genuine laughter to lighten the atmosphere at least somewhat.

"I've always wanted to do that," he announced, pleased with himself, "but somehow an occasion for champagne never came up before this."

With a flourish, he filled the two gracefully fluted glasses the hotel had provided and brought them over to her. "We're acting like a coupla idiots, you know," he said, handing her a glass.

His dryly conversational tone made Roni smile. "I know."

"I vote we stop it right now."

"Me, too."

He moved closer. His gaze heating, he touched the rim of his glass to hers. "I want to make a toast, Veronica...."

Roni's heart was doing a crazy tomtom act. Expecting him to toast the occasion, she was surprised and not a little disconcerted to hear him solemnly say, "To you, Veronica Sykes, the most generous and giving woman I have ever met."

Touched, but embarrassed, too, Roni shook her head and raised her own glass. "And I want to drink to you, Gerald Marsden. A man of courage and compassion who deserves all the very best in life."

Courage and compassion? Him? He was scared to death of everything that had been happening and daily calling himself a fool for not having gotten the boy out of his life by now.

Uncomfortable and feeling like a fraud, Gerald withstood Roni's warm, serious gaze with some difficulty, and when she had taken the sip that convention decreed, hurried to forestall any further kudos by taking her glass and firmly setting it down. He did the same with his own and, determined to get past their hang-ups and introduce some measure of romance into this night he'd had such high hopes for, held out his hands.

"Let's dance."

Unable to switch gears quite so fast, Roni hesitated with a nervous little laugh. "But there's no music."

"Doesn't matter." He took her hands and drew her close. "Since I don't know how to dance." Putting his arms around her and his cheek to hers, he began to sway back and forth.

Charmed, disarmed, Roni smiled, closed her eyes and melted into Gerald and his movements.

"This is nice, don't you think?" he asked after a bit, nuzzling her cheek.

"Hmm…" Roni could swear that a string quartet was playing softly just for them. "Do you hear the same music I'm hearing?"

"I must be." His lips grazed her ear. "We're moving in harmony, aren't we?"

"Hmm…" Were they ever. Roni arched her throat, giving access to Gerald's gently exploring lips, the sensations caused by the brushing of thigh against thigh, belly against belly stoking the glow of want into flame.

"I like how we move."

Kisses were feathered along her jaw. "Yes…"

The zip at the back of her dress came down and warm hands slid inside for a flat-palmed exploration. The movements of their dance slowed and became more intimate as one of those hands insinuated itself into the top of her panty hose and pressed against the small of her back, urging her hips into alignment with his.

"I want you, Roni."

Even without that husky declaration, body to body as they were, Veronica would have known. He was all man and rigid, and everything that was woman inside her eagerly responded. "Hmm…"

"We're married now…." He stopped moving and, when Roni a little reluctantly lifted her head off his shoulder, looked deeply into her eyes. "I want to make love with you."

The words, *make love,* came with some difficulty, and Gerald said them only because he knew they were necessary. All he really wanted—needed—from this woman in his arms was sex, pure and simple.

"I won't hurt you, Roni...."

Yes, you will, Roni thought, following his moves, melting into him, and determined to take all she could get from him on this magical night of nights.

"I'll take care of you, sweetheart." He rocked her, stroked her, stoked the smoldering fires into ravaging flames. He undressed her, caressed her, inflamed her, murmuring, "Don't worry, I'll take care of things. Nothing will happen but you and me being good to each other...."

Having sex. Good sex. Hot sex. The best...

Except, as Roni wordlessly acquiesced and became still more pliant in his arms, as he touched his lips to hers and was rocked again by the explosive charge their kisses never failed to unleash and felt her heart beating fast and furious against his, it wasn't sex that was on Gerald's mind, it was love.

Unfamiliar and unrecognized, if he had known the feeling for what it was, he would have vehemently denied and fought against it. But he didn't consciously realize that it was love with which he stroked Veronica into passion, love with which he worshiped at her breasts, and love with which he brought his wife to a shuddering reward and followed her up to the stars. All he realized, briefly, as passion exploded into a mind-shattering release, was that sex had never before been this good.

Somehow, Roni fuzzily realized much later, they had gotten undressed. Somehow they'd ended up on the bed, if not beneath the sheets. And somehow—wondrously, magically—she had been made to feel beautiful and utterly desirable by the man who lay spent and sprawled half on top of her.

Was he—could he possibly have fallen asleep?

Drawing back a little, Roni squinted into her new husband's face and was struck by the defenseless boyishness of his handsome features in repose. A wave of tenderness and love engulfing her, she touched his cheek in a phantom caress.

Her husband. Her love. She kissed him, feather-light, on the mouth.

As if she had taken a vicious bite out of him instead of bestowing a gentle kiss, Gerald's face contorted in a spasm of pain and, muttering something harsh, short and incoherent, he jerked himself off her and rolled onto his feet. Splendidly naked and seemingly oblivious to her presence, his back rigid and shoulders set, he crossed the room and disappeared into the bathroom.

The door shut loudly, and with a finality that made it clear to Roni that she'd just been evicted from whatever private spot inside of Gerald she had all too briefly been allowed to enter. Staring at the closed panel, she shivered and, drawing up her knees, hugged herself against a chill that had nothing to do with ambient temperatures and everything to do with fear.

Fear that the inevitable heartache would start so much sooner than she'd expected—hoped. Fear that her dreams for the future would be dashed before she'd even had a chance to show Gerald how good life with a wife and child could be. Fear that she might have failed to give as much joy as she had received here on their wedding bed, and that Gerald was rejecting her.

Cold with misery, she hovered on the bed, listening to the sound of Gerald's shower and wondering how in the world she could bear to face him when he came out.

And then she thought, hearing Aunt Lou's voice, *Well, for starters, missy, you can stop cowering like some sorry little wimp on this bed.* And almost smiled.

Electrified with purpose, she rushed over to the sofa where her overnight bag still reposed. With hands that shook from nervous haste now, not fear, she unzipped the thing and tugged out the garments she had earlier so carefully and self-consciously folded into it. A sheer, body skimming gown and matching peignoir.

Keeping an ear tuned for sounds from the bathroom, she rushed over to the mirror, took sufficient note of her tumbled hair and kiss-swollen lips to profusely blush, and shimmied the gown over her head.

Wow. Smoothing shaky hands over narrow hips, Roni stared in disbelief at the siren's shape in shimmeringly translucent ivory silk. This couldn't be her...could it? Stepping back a pace, half turning this way and that, pulling in the tummy, sticking out the chest and, with a stifled giggle of delight, letting everything settle back into place, she thought, Yes. Yes, it's me. It's *me!*

And told herself that if Gerald found her lacking the first time around—in this, looking sexy and feeling determined, with the whole night ahead of them, she'd do her darnedest not to be found lacking the next.

The sound of running water stopped and, quickly now, Roni shrugged into the peignoir. With its filmy nothingness floating behind her like gossamer wings, she hurried back to the bed. There she threw back the spread, propped up the pillows and arranged herself against them in what she hoped was an alluring sort of half-reclining position. She only had time to fluff her hair and spread one fall of it over her bosom, before the bathroom door opened.

Since his duffel was still in the sitting area where he'd dropped it what seemed like a lifetime ago, Gerald was forced to exit the bathroom pretty much the same way he had entered it—naked. Which was what he did, except for the bath towel he'd tucked around his hips and which fell, like an abbreviated sarong, to below his knees.

Which still left a most impressive spread of chest and belly free to be viewed and admired by Veronica, who did so as best she could while striving to look dreamily at ease and trying not to be obvious as she ogled. She had decided to be laid-back, relaxed, for the time being, and to let Gerald set the tone for the next few minutes.

Catching sight of Roni on the bed, Gerald stopped as if struck in the bathroom door. His eyes did a rapid scan of her languidly recumbent form, flaring with heat—both new and remembered—as they briefly connected with hers.

And then, jerking his gaze away from hers as abruptly as he'd earlier jerked himself off her body, he marched toward the couch like a soldier into battle—grim-faced, eyes straight ahead, chin jutted out like a banner of war.

Roni watched his determined progress, with butterflies doing a dance in her stomach and with her heart in her throat. How forbidding he looked. How unapproachable. She had to be crazy to think— But wait . . .

About halfway to the couch, Gerald suddenly stopped. *Moose Marsden, you insensitive idiot, you've got an attitude problem that won't quit, and the only people you're hurting are yourself and the woman you know deserves better.* The starch went out of his shoulders. They sagged. Slowly, slowly, he turned around.

Standing there, his expression no longer grim, but troubled, he forced himself to look into Veronica's face. He knew that somehow he'd have to make her understand what it was with him, why her tenderness in the aftermath of their passion had frightened him so. Why this whole scene, so different from any other sexual encounter he'd had, scared the hell out of him.

Roni met Gerald's anguished gaze as levelly as she was able, given the turmoil of her own emotions, and waited for him to speak.

When finally he did, his voice was rough, as though rusty from disuse. "I'm...sorry," he said, and Roni got the impression from some tiny, involuntary muscle movement, that he wanted very much to come to her. "I'm sorry...."

Awash with love and sympathy for this proud man who was humbling himself for her, Roni wordlessly opened her arms to him.

And, just as wordlessly, Gerald came into them.

"It's never been like that for me before," he confessed. With his face pressed into her neck, the words were muffled, but Roni heard and soothingly stroked his hair. "I..." She felt him swallow and kissed the top of his head the way a mother does a hurt child. "You don't know how it's been all my life...."

"Then tell me," Roni whispered, her throat such an ache, it hurt to breathe, much less speak. "Help me to understand...."

She felt his muscles bunch as he prepared to pull out of her embrace, but she said, "Stay," and held him more tightly.

Gerald knew he'd be leaving himself wide open to hurt and humiliation with what he was about to do. The urge to pull away, to withdraw on all fronts and shut down again, was almost overwhelming. It was a measure of his respect and . . . *regard* for this woman whose fragrant warmth enveloped him like a benediction, that he forced himself to relax. To stay. And to try.

She had been so wonderful to . . . love, this woman whom he once had thought plain and who now seemed to him the most beautiful creature on earth. This woman who was now the wife he never wanted. Whom—God help him, he still didn't want, except in that one, that glorious way. . . .

He almost laughed then, and bitterly thought, Who was he kidding? He was getting in deeper than he'd ever wanted to be, in over his head and drowning, and it was the scariest thing he'd ever come up against.

Restless, and unable to stay nestled against Veronica any longer, Gerald straightened and gently disengaged himself from her embrace.

Filled with sorrow, thinking the interlude over and the moment of closeness past, Roni let him go.

But Gerald only needed to move, to pace, as he struggled to wrestle the words out of a recalcitrant mind and hesitantly exposed them to Roni's judgment and— hopefully—understanding.

"All my life I've seen women as the enemy," he said. "I hated my mother, hated and feared anything female. Except Marcy . . ."

"Pete's mom."

Gerald nodded. "She was different." He paced. "Always before, with women, I felt like they took from me, disenfranchised me. They were always the ones with the power. They decided, arbitrarily from my point of view, who I would be, where I should live, how and with whom. They decreed where I could and couldn't go. But Marcy was different. With her it was just the opposite.

She was the helpless one. I was the one with the power—"

"Funny you didn't abuse it," Roni interrupted musingly, "as a means of getting even."

Surprised, Gerald stared at her. "That's what the prison shrink said, too."

"And?"

"And I'll tell you the same thing I told him—'What do you take me for, some kind of brute?'"

"No." In one graceful motion, Roni was off the bed and walking toward him. "I think," she said, pleased with the way Gerald's eyes visibly widened at the sight of her silken splendor in spite of her empathetic concentration on his words. "I think that you're a very sensitive, very caring man who is afraid—"

"Afraid?" Disconcerted by Roni's alluring proximity as well as by her remarkable perception, Gerald made a scornful sound. "Don't kid yourself, lady."

"Afraid to trust in the caring and sensitivity of others," Roni finished calmly.

"Yeah, well..." Needing to do something, Gerald went to the couch and rummaged through his duffel. "Maybe. It's kept me from getting my feelings stepped on, though, I tell you."

"Has it?" Roni challenged softly. "Has it really?"

This was getting too heavy. She was getting too close, much closer than he was ready to let anyone get, even her. Yanking a pair of sweats out of the duffel and stepping into them before ripping the towel off his waist and tossing it aside, Gerald glared at Roni. "I did the shrink bit in prison, all right? So please spare me the amateur analysis...."

He stalked to the window and stared out. Darkness had fallen. In the distance, the state capitol had been transformed into an amber sphere from the footlights that illuminated it. Faint traffic noises were audible. Farther out, the freeway was a blackish snake, dotted with moving pinpoints of lights, both white and red. Cars, people, coming and going. Where to? Where from?

And where the hell had he wanted this conversation with Veronica to go, anyway? Not to this stalemate, that was for sure.

"Look, Veronica..." He turned around to face her again and was struck by how lovely she looked, and felt more inadequate than ever. "Maybe this wasn't such a good idea...."

"What?" Roni quipped with glibness she was far from feeling. "Our getting married?"

He gave a short laugh. "I think that goes without saying. But no—" He sobered into grimness. "I meant this...this—"

"Baring of the soul?"

"Yeah." He scowled down at the carpet, raking a hand through his hair. "Yeah. It's not something I'm very good at, or enjoy."

"Nobody does." Wanting to help him so badly, she ached with it, Roni walked up to him and laid a hand on his arm, taking heart when he only looked down at it instead of brushing it off. "But you know something, Gerald? There's no shame in it, not when you do it with someone who cares." *As much as I do,* she added mentally.

He raised his head then and let his eyes meet hers. The caring she spoke of was there for him to see, and something else, something softer, deeper, something that made his breath catch and his heart skip a beat— that was there, too.

"Roni..." Of its own accord, his hand reached out and curved itself around her cheek and jaw. "Do you have any idea how special you are?" he said hoarsely as she laid her own hand over his. "It's one of the things I've been trying to tell you in my clumsy, self-pitying way—"

"No." Roni laid a finger across his mouth to silence him. "None of that."

"I've never known a woman like you," Gerald continued, removing her hand but keeping it clasped in his. "You're neither like Marcy nor like any of the others. You're—"

"I'm *me,*" Roni said quietly. "That's all."

"No." Gerald's voice became low and husky as he tugged her closer. "Never say 'that's all.' You're more, so much more, than I—any man—has a right to expect.

"Shh..." he said, when, shaking her head, Roni opened her mouth to demur. "Let me say this. I know I'll probably be a bastard to live with more often than not. Things get to me—just as they did a while ago after we..."

He faltered, but his gaze on Roni's stayed true. "After we made love. But I want you to know it's got nothing to do with you. It's me, Veronica. A lot of stuff's been coming at me in an awful hurry here lately, and it's taking me some time to get used to...to things being different than they were. So never think that it's you, darlin'...."

He kissed her lips, lightly, sweetly, and smiled tenderly into her eyes. "Never think it's you...."

Chapter Ten

They had made love again that night—sweetly, slowly, without the urgency and wildness of their first melding, but with a passion that was as tender as it was all-consuming. And this time, afterward, Gerald had clamped down on the urge to run and had held Veronica the way she needed and deserved to be held and cherished.

They had talked some more, soft murmurings, bits of self-revelation, only this time Roni had been the one to do most of the opening up. She had told Gerald of her parents, who had died so tragically and so young. Both marine biologists, they had been diving off the coast of Australia as part of a research team and had been killed by a shark attack. Though Roni hadn't been told the gruesome details of their deaths until well in her teens, she'd been left with a fear of the ocean her parents would have strongly lamented.

Roni had been only five when she'd been orphaned. And it had taken her years to understand that her parents hadn't abandoned her, hadn't simply gone off on one of their frequent trips and reneged on their promise to see her again soon.

George and Louise had had their hands full with the moody adolescent and surly teen Roni had been, but their love and devotion, their seemingly boundless patience and willingness to forgive had, in the end—

Here Roni had laughed a little self-consciously and burrowed her face into the crook of Gerald's neck. —shamed her into becoming a halfway decent and upstanding citizen. From a person who'd been obsessed with "poor little me," she had gradually, and often painfully, matured and metamorphosed into someone whose first thought invariably was "What can I do for you?"

Which came as no news to Gerald, of course, since he'd certainly been, and still was, on the receiving end of Roni's generous and giving attitude. Encouraged by Veronica's openness, sucked into the moment that seemed to invite the sharing of confidences, Gerald, too, had lowered his guard enough to talk about his past. About prison. And about how he'd gotten there.

"I never killed anyone in my life," he told Roni, willing her to believe him, needing her to know he'd been wild in those days but not really rotten. "All I did that day was *be* there in that liquor store. Strength in numbers and all that crap. Can you believe that?"

Roni had nodded, her eyes filled with emotions he couldn't bear—didn't dare—to decipher and interpret, but which deep down he knew were special and honest and, as they pertained to him, as rare as the most precious gems.

He told her briefly of Big Mike who had killed his wife and children in a fit of drunken rage but who, to Gerald, had been the closest thing to a father he'd probably ever have. Big Mike was a lot like Judge Cunningham, come to think of it, Gerald told Roni, and if it'd been possible for him to love anyone, then Big Mike would've been the one man he would have loved.

But—and here he'd forced himself to chuckle and drop a kiss on Roni's nose—love was only for storybooks and fairy tales.

Roni, aghast, had held him tight and cried.

No one had ever cried for Gerald before. Not like that. Nor had they held him like Roni had held him, or loved him the way she had done. She was special, this wife of his he didn't really want, and he despised himself thoroughly and totally when, after Roni had fallen asleep, he found himself unable to stay close to her, after all. He got up out of bed, dressed and snuck out of the room like a thief in the night.

Walking the streets, wrestling with demons he'd thought he'd put to rest in the course of his psychotherapy in prison, the realization emerged that it wasn't women per se he distrusted and feared, nor was it commitment, filial responsibility or even the loss of his freedom. No, the thing he was afraid of was love.

Love was an alien emotion he had experienced only once, in that foster home aeons ago. He had loved those people, and he'd been devastated when the state had stepped in and removed him from their care.

He'd never known his mother. He'd been only hours old when she'd left him in a police station parking lot, and so she was really just a concept. And, walking the nearly deserted streets of Salem, Gerald came to understand that it was this concept—the *knowledge* of her betrayal—that he had spent all these years hating. His mother's abandonment of him had been painful only in the abstract—how can you miss what you never knew?—but to be forcefully separated from those loving foster parents had been very real. The experience had killed something in Gerald. It had killed the ability to love.

Or so he had thought until Pete. And Veronica.

Having come full circle, the darkness of the night fading as dawn painted the sky in hues of orange, lilac and red, Gerald stood in front of the ornate facade of the Carlton Hotel and stared up at the window he thought might be their room. His heart was heavy.

Behind him, the street was coming alive with commuters who didn't have Sundays off and were driving their cars to work. A bus rumbled past, leaving the smell of diesel in its wake. From the hotel restaurant delicious morning smells teased Gerald's nostrils—freshly brewed coffee, still-warm rolls and breads. Bacon.

Gerald's stomach rumbled, reminding him that it had been quite some time since yesterday's light wedding supper. And still he stood, petrified by the revelation that the ability to love had not been killed in him at all, it had only been dormant.

And that the woman up there behind the window he was so intently staring at, had called it to life.

He jerked his gaze off the building, went so far as to turn his back on it, in fact, as if by doing so he could turn his back on Veronica, as well. Which was exactly what he needed to do, if he were to have any chance of getting out of the tangled web some capricious fate had decided to weave for him. He didn't want to feel anything deep for Veronica Sykes; he couldn't handle the kind of emotional upheaval that seemed to be the inevitable by-product of love. He'd been totally messed up by that first loss years ago; to lose again would destroy him.

So why take the chance? Who needed more heartache? Not him, that was for sure; he'd had about all the misery he'd care to have in one lifetime. So keep your distance, Marsden, he told himself. Put a lid on it. And get the hell out of *her* life and *this* mess while you've still got a chance.

"Gerald...?" Stretching luxuriantly, feeling wonderful, Roni came awake slowly and with a smile. She was married to a pretty terrific man, she was in love and she had just spent the most glorious night of her life in the arms of her lover.

Languidly Roni rolled her head to the side, her heartbeat already picking up speed in anticipation of the sight of him, only to have it falter at the sight of tossed back sheets and a dented pillow...and a yawningly empty expanse of mattress.

He was gone.

Roni shot upright, and immediately subsided back against her pillow with a feeling of chagrin. The bathroom, silly. He's in the bathroom.

A giggle rose into her throat and was stifled as she buried her face in the pillow and good-naturedly scolded herself. You're going to have to cut out the melodrama, kid, or you'll drive yourself—and your husband—crazy.

Husband. Roni hugged the word to herself with a dreamy smile. Gerald...

Rolling onto her back again, she listened for the shower. Hearing nothing, she tensed. He'd be out in a minute.

Suddenly conscious of the fact that she generally looked like the wrath of God first thing in the morning, Roni sprang from the bed, scooped her nightgown up off the floor and dragged it on over her head as she rushed to the mirror.

Aw, heck. Thoroughly disgusted, Roni closed her eyes a moment and wondered why it was that in books and in the movies, brides were always beautifully radiant the morning after while she looked as if someone had attacked her hair with an eggbeater and kneaded her face as if it were a ball of putty.

Blowing a hard breath of displeasure out through her teeth, Roni brought her face close to the glass and with her fingertips tugged the outer corners of her eyes upward and out.

Sucking in her cheeks, she uttered in a vampish manner, "Much better, dahlink," before, with an exasperated snort, she let everything go and stuck her tongue out at herself. "Idiot..."

Turning her back on the mirror, she finger-combed the worst tangles out of her hair and was just slipping her arms into the sleeves of her peignoir, when the door opened and Gerald walked in.

Except it wasn't the bathroom door through which he came into the room.

Surprise kept Roni momentarily motionless, but then she mentally shrugged—So he'd gone out. So what?— and, with a glad cry, rushed to meet and welcome him. "Gerald...! Good mor—"

Something was wrong. With his suit rumpled, his tieless shirt unbuttoned three down, Gerald looked haggard, tired and, once again, grim.

"—ning," she finished lamely.

"Hi." Barely sparing Roni a glance, aware that he was being cruel, but at a loss as to how else to keep her at arm's length, Gerald headed straight for the bathroom. "Whyn't you order us some coffee while I grab a quick shower. I want to get out of here as soon as possible."

"But—" Checkout time wasn't till noon, and she'd hoped...

"I've got to get to work."

"Work?" Gerald wasn't due back at the construction site until further notice—they'd been hit by a strike—and the plan was for him to take advantage of this time off and apply at some of the architectural firms in town. "But this is Sunday and—"

"Yeah, well," he muttered, "there's still stuff to be done in the attic...."

The rest of his mumbled explanation was drowned out by the closing of the bathroom door, done with the same firm finality of the night before. As she had been then, Roni was left staring at its cold whiteness with dread spreading through her like a cancer.

Something was wrong. Again. He was shutting her out. Again. And she'd been left to wonder in which way she was lacking. Again.

For a moment she almost bought into that, and then she thought, No, dammit, not this time! And marched into the bathroom after him.

Surprised to hear the door flying open, Gerald swiveled his head in time to see Roni sweep into the room like one of the legendary Furies.

"All right," she announced in ringing tones and with emerald eyes ablaze, "what's going on?"

Keeping his face carefully blank, Gerald merely cocked a brow and went back to removing his socks with a calm nonchalance that was strictly for show.

Roni, livid, punched him in the shoulder and made him lose his balance, forcing him to set his foot down and straighten. "I'd like an answer," she said seething, "if you don't mind."

"An answer to what?" Play dumb, Moose, why don't ya!

He only had his briefs on, Roni belatedly noted, caressing his muscled form with her eyes even as she wanted to throttle him. He was magnificent, this new husband of hers, and during the night they'd just shared, she'd come to know the might and strength of him exquisitely well. He had pleasured her with that body, and had praised her for pleasuring him.

But now... Now he was looking at her as dispassionately as at a stranger.

Her ire shriveled as suddenly as it had bloomed. This was no replay of last night's brief withdrawal from her, she realized bleakly. He intended this to be much more serious, much more final. An immense sadness filled her heart. But though she wanted to reach for him and plead with him to give it—her—time and a chance, she only achingly whispered, "Why?"

Gerald, standing stoically before her, was bleeding inside, too. The sight of Roni's bewildered hurt was tearing him up, and yet all he could do—*had* to do— was to stick by his attitude and to keep up the shield he'd worked to put in place in the course of his long nocturnal walk. If he let her tear down that shield just once again, he'd never be able to build it anew. And that was just too risky.

"Look, Veronica," he said quietly. "I know you don't understand—hell I'm not even sure I get it myself—and I'm sorry I'm acting like such a jerk here, but the truth is, I tried but I just can't do this intimacy scene."

Unable to endure her somber scrutiny, he turned his back on the pain that was clouding her eyes, yanked open the shower door and turned the faucets on full blast.

"What we got here is a marriage of convenience that'll be terminated just as soon as is humanly possible," he said, talking into the shower stall. "And I've decided it'd be best for all concerned if we kept things strictly business in the meantime."

"I see."

It was the quiet dignity with which she replied that undid him. With a vicious curse, his shoulders slumped and his head dropped to his chest. "Aw, hell, Veronica," he said heavily. "Who'm I kidding? The truth o' the matter is . . ."

He turned to look into her face as he said the words, *"I've fallen in love with you and it scares me to death."* But Roni was no longer there.

More than anything, it had been Gerald's harsh expletive that had convinced Roni that she didn't want to hear anything else he might have to say to her just then.

She had gotten his message loud and clear—in spite of the progress they'd made in terms of coming closer to each other, or maybe *because* of it, Gerald Marsden considered last night an aberration and a mistake.

Given the strength of her own feelings for Gerald, Roni should have been devastated by this latest reversal, but she had gotten another message, too. Gerald's cold words and aloof demeanor notwithstanding, making that declaration had caused him pain. The knowledge went a long way toward easing the hurt Roni was feeling, and it kept alive in her the hope that maybe with time, and care, and tolerance...

Oh, hell. Veronica heaved a sigh and began gathering up her things so that she could nip into the bathroom the moment Gerald came out. Maybe she was kidding herself, but she wasn't a quitter, and she'd been so sure last night that they were good together. Still, she'd be lying if she said she wasn't feeling lousy....

Gerald emerged from the bathroom, halfway covered again in a towel, and without speaking, Roni brushed past him for her own shower. His lips compressed, brows low, Gerald got himself dressed in the jeans and polo shirt he'd brought and told himself it was a lucky thing Veronica hadn't hung around to listen to the fool thing he'd been about to admit. Talk about bringing your own rope to a hanging!

One thing was certain, he had to get things resolved, and get out of this marriage and that boardinghouse, pronto. Because there was no way he'd be able to spend any amount of time around Roni without eventually spilling his guts about his feelings for her. And nothing good could come of that. So, first thing next week he'd go and light a fire under that private dick he'd hired.

On the way home, in the taxi, Roni and Gerald agreed to put up a good front for Aunt Lou, Pete and the boarders. Nothing too mushy, just friendly civility of the sort they imagined married people exhibited to-

ward each other. A peck on the cheek now and then—
surely they could both manage that? The nights might
be a bit more awkward, though, mightn't they? After
all, they'd be sharing the bedroom. But the bed in it was
a king and surely two people could sleep on that without...

Yes.

They both looked elsewhere and rushed past that
point.

"Hey, you guys!" Peter was out of the boardinghouse door and in Roni's arms the minute the cab
pulled away from the curb. She hugged him tightly,
fighting the tears that had rushed to her eyes and struggling to hang on to a smile.

"Hi, sweetie," she said, drawing back a little to gaze
into his freckled face. "Did you look after things all
right around here?"

"Yup!" Done with greetings, Pete seemed impatient
to be done with the mushy stuff, too. "An' Leo gave me
a bath 'n Miz Henks read me a story 'n Aunt Lou and I
made cookies 'n..."

As Peter rambled on, Roni's eyes went to Louise who
was walking toward them more sedately, drying her
hands on her apron, beaming, before enfolding Gerald
in as big a hug as their size differential allowed.

She'd be hitting him over the head if she knew of our
recent reversal, Roni thought with bittersweet affection
for the two people she loved most in the world.

"...but I'm glad you're home again anyway," Peter was finishing his recital, and, pressing a fervent kiss
onto his cheek before letting him go, Roni revised her
thought to, Two of the *three* people she loved most in
the world.

In a fervent prayer, she added, Please, God, don't let them find 'Nana' Kemp.

But her prayer was not about to be answered.

Blinded by tears, Roni stared out at the street and the ugly purple house beyond. One foot was folded beneath her, the tip of her other one touched the floor now and then to keep the porch swing gently swaying. The motion should have soothed her, but didn't. She was wound as tight as a watch spring and ready to snap at the first person daring to invade the privacy she'd come out here to find.

With a houseful of well-meaning people, it was sometimes difficult to find a place where one could grieve alone, though tonight, Roni suspected, each of the other occupants of the house had sought out his or her own sanctuary, too.

Because at dinner that night, Gerald had said, "Can you believe it? Only my second interview with Mirashki Architects and Design and they want me to come aboard as a designer."

"Really?" chorused the elderly ladies.

"Good man!" and, "'Course we can believe it!" from Leo and the judge.

Roni hadn't even tried to keep the pride she took in Gerald, nor the wealth of love she felt for him, out of her smile. For the first time since their wedding night ten days ago she had unguardedly met Gerald's gaze as she quietly told him, "I think this is just about the most wonderful thing I've heard."

The *most* wonderful thing having been Gerald's telling her how much he wanted her.

But she was determined not to let that kind of musing spoil the moment. Squelching all but the most positive emotions, she held his gaze and her own happy smile. "Congratulations, Gerald."

But instead of smiling back and happily acknowledging her and everybody else's felicitations and delight, Gerald's eyes had clouded beneath a gathering scowl.

"Aren't you happy?" she had asked him, puzzled by his demeanor.

He had nodded. Keeping her trapped in a moody stare, he'd said, "I have other news, too, though."

"Oh?" Something cold had wrapped itself around Roni's heart. With a sense of foreboding, she'd asked, "What is it?"

"The boy's grandmother lives in a trailer of some kind in Barstow, California."

The announcement exploded into the happy dinner table gathering like an atom bomb, causing everyone's stunned gaze to fly to Gerald in the devastated silence which followed.

Everyone's but Roni's. Her first concern was for Peter, and her horrified gaze shot toward him, wondering at his reaction, worrying—

But she needn't have worried. The boy was blessedly intent on his second helping of tapioca pudding—his favorite—which Judge Cunningham had snuck to him with the not entirely true declaration that he was too full to eat it himself, and wasn't paying attention to the adult conversation around him.

"What are you going to do?" Roni had asked then, directing her attention back to Gerald, and more than a little surprised that she was even able to speak past the dread that was strangling her vocal chords. "Will you be taking him . . . back?"

He hadn't answered right away, and the silence had hung in the room like a leaden shroud. Darkly he had studied Peter. The boy had looked up, pudding smears around his mouth, and grinned at Gerald who had quickly averted his gaze and stared down at his plate.

"You knew," he'd finally said to the room at large, but not looking at any of them. They'd all been silent observers these past ten days of the strained relations between Roni and himself, but whatever their thoughts on the matter, they'd tactfully kept them to themselves. Now, too, no one said a word, but somehow Gerald found that harder to bear than their most outraged protestations.

"You *all* knew good and well what the deal was," he'd told them grimly. "Nothing's changed."

Nothing's changed.

Now, sitting alone in the semidarkness of the porch, Roni felt bitter laughter rise into her throat, and she pressed a hand to her lips to keep it contained. For ten days she'd hoped for change. Every day. Every night, lying next to him on that bed, physically close yet feeling emotionally farther removed from him than she'd felt even in the beginning of their acquaintance. And, every morning waking up in his arms, instinctively turning to him in the night before awkwardly moving away from him in the morning. She'd hoped that in time, *given* time, Gerald would come to trust her again, and would maybe grow to love her. But now—

Dammit, everything had changed once again! But not for the better, and once too often!

Where was that man? Bent on confrontation, Roni jumped off the swing and marched into the house. Gerald was in none of the rooms she checked, but she'd been right—having been relieved of the job of keeping up a cheerful front with Peter in bed, Aunt Lou and the others had withdrawn to ponder and mourn this latest turn of events in their respective corners of the house.

Roni found Gerald in her uncle George's workshop behind the house. He was putting the finishing touches on a soapbox car he and Peter had been building for the past couple of weeks.

"Not much point in finishing that, is there?" Roni asked, her tone as brittle and cool as glass.

Gerald didn't look up from the piece he was sanding "He can take it home with him."

"Home?" Roni felt her voice rise an octave and took a deep breath. "Gerald, *this* is Peter's home, right here with us."

He faced her then, his expression set. "Until the grandmother was found, Veronica. That was the deal."

His calm obduracy infuriated her. "Dammit, we're talking about a child here, not some lifeless, faceless...*thing* you make deals about. For heaven's sake, Gerald, the boy loves us, he's happy here—"

"And before that, he loved his nana and was happy with her," Gerald interrupted with his own head of steam building up. "He's not my son, Veronica—"

"Isn't he?"

"You know damn well he's not!"

"Of the flesh, no, he isn't." Roni walked up to the workbench and trailed a finger along the sleek body of the soapbox car. "But in all the ways that matter..."

"Dammit!" Gerald exploded, driving a fist into the nearest wall, thus rattling the tools that hung there. "Don't do this to me!"

Pacing, he raked a hand through his hair and, his face contorting into a grimace of pain and frustration, shot

Roni a fulminating glare. "Do you think this is easy for me?"

"Then why *do* it?" Roni cried. "Gerald, please..."

"Because I have to, dammit! I *have* to!" Nearly beside himself—did she have to look at him as if he were the Boston Strangler?—Gerald gripped Roni's upper arms and gave her a hard shake. "It's him or me, don't you see? If I don't take him back, if I keep him, it's just one more time that I'm stuck in a situation I had no hand in creating. All my life I've been trapped and manipulated by other people, and I've had it with that."

Roughly letting her go, almost shoving her away, he turned away. "After I got out of prison, *I* was gonna be the only guy who ever called the shots in my life again. But now look at me—"

His voice dropped and roughened with scorn. "—stuck with a kid I didn't make and a wife I never wanted...."

Roni didn't hear anything else. As if pursued by the demons straight from hell, she ran out of the workshop.

Chapter Eleven

Two beds, a table and two chairs. Spots on the worn, once-red carpet, clear plastic covers over lamp shades that no longer merited such protection—this was Room 313 of the Shady Grove Motel in some nameless speck on the map just off Highway 99 in central California. Gerald looked around the room before returning to the car for Pete.

Wanting to make time, wanting to economize by not having to fork out more than one night's lodging, *wanting to get this odious mission over with as quickly as possible,* Gerald had spent eighteen hours on the road. He was driving the aged blue Chevy sedan he'd bought for seven hundred dollars just a few days earlier. So far, it seemed the seller had been right—while not much to look at, the car was reliable transportation.

Pulling up in front of his motel unit, gazing at Pete who had lost the battle against increasing somnolence soon after the fast-food dinner they'd eaten some two hundred miles earlier, Gerald slumped behind the wheel for a minute and expelled a weary breath. This was hell.

And the days leading up to this one had been no better. Roni's silent misery and unbending reproach, the unhappiness of Louise Upshot and the boarders, which their pitiful attempts at cheery optimism and unbiased support had made all the more difficult to bear. And Peter.

The little guy's hurt bewilderment had defied both Gerald's and Roni's attempts at explanations. Roni, to give her credit, had not allowed her own pain and bitterness toward Gerald to deter her from trying to make Pete understand what she herself could not—namely that a return to his nana would be the best thing Gerald could do for him.

Pete hadn't understood—and he still didn't—beyond the fact that he was no longer wanted by the dad he'd come to love, and that he wasn't allowed to stay any longer with his adored Veronica and with the old folks who'd become his family. He'd been so excited, so proud, to finally have a room all his own in the attic. To have a mom and dad just like the other kids, and a whole bunch of "grandparents," too.

Watching the boy lose the shine and sparkle he'd acquired over the past few months and seeing him revert to pale-faced sullenness was murder. It, on top of Roni's coldness and everybody else's down-at-the-mouth attitude, had been almost more than Gerald could endure.

And yet, endure it he must and did, for what choice did he have? If he was to have any chance at all at the kind of freewheeling, go-where-you-want, unfettered-by-responsibilities-to-others kind of life he'd planned out for himself during his years in prison, he couldn't be saddled with a wife and kid.

It would've been one thing if he'd been so stupid as to get someone like Veronica Sykes pregnant. He'd have hated himself for his carelessness but he'd have done the right thing and married her, and too bad about other plans. It would've been his own fault then that his dreams had gone up in smoke.

But things weren't like that here. He *hadn't* been stupid, he *hadn't* knocked anybody up. He *wasn't* this kid's old man and the only reason he'd married Veronica Sykes was because some third person—Marcy Kemp—had been too dumb to keep her knees together when it counted, and naive enough to think any father was better than none.

Well, Marcy had been wrong. Or, at least, she'd been wrong when she'd stuck him with the honor. He hadn't agreed to it. He didn't want it. He couldn't hack it.

All his life, it seemed to Gerald, other people—most of them female—had decided how things were going to be. Thanks to them, things had been the pits most of the time. Now, dammit, it was his turn to call the shots and nobody—not the boarders, not Pete and not even Veronica Sykes—was going to keep him from calling them. His way.

Exhausted—physically from the grueling drive, and emotionally from the relentless beating-up he'd been giving himself—Gerald carried Pete into the motel room, tucked him into bed and, moments later, was himself sleeping like the dead.

He came awake what seemed like only minutes later to bright sunshine flooding the room and Peter, sitting cross-legged on the bed next to his, fixedly regarding him with solemn, chocolate-colored eyes.

"Whatsa matter?" Blinking grit from his eyes and roughly swiping a hand across his stubbled face, Gerald wearily struggled to a sitting position against the headboard. "Time's it?"

He glanced at his watch: 8:07. *Jeez...* In a hurry now, Gerald surged off the bed, cursing himself for sleeping in, thinking that at this rate he'd still have the kid in tow by tonight. Grabbing up his jeans, he headed for the bathroom.

"Dad . . . ?"

Pete's hesitant call arrested his steps. With the sound of the word—*Dad*—humming bittersweetly within him, Gerald slowly turned. "What?"

Seeing Pete's face crumble, he silently swore. He hadn't meant to sound so gruff, but there was pain in his throat and his heart ached and he couldn't stop despising himself for what he was doing to this confused and forlorn little boy who demanded so little of him— and yet so much more than he was able to give.

With an effort, Gerald moderated his tone. "What is it, son? We're in a hurry. . . ."

He could see it cost the kid to speak, just as it was costing him. The little chin ducked down, wobbling, and the boy's voice was thick with tears as, after a couple of dry runs, he finally said, "How come you don't love me no more, Dad?"

A bullet through the heart would have been more welcome to Gerald than the dagger thrust of Pete's plaintive query. Sweet Mother Murphy, he thought, letting his own chin drop to his chest as his fisted hand tightened around the denim of his jeans like a vise. What in *hell* could he say to that? What could he tell the boy, how could he explain? He couldn't, but he'd damn well better try.

In a flash, Gerald was on his knees in front of the small, huddling form and, urging the quivering chin up with one finger, peered intently into the downcast eyes.

"It's not like that, Pete," he said gently. "This isn't about loving you or not—"

"Nana said you're my dad..."

Damn the woman. Damn Marcy.

"This isn't about that, either, son." *Son.* Gerald felt something twist inside. How easily the word rolled off his tongue. How right it had become to use in connection with Peter. And how increasingly easy it was becoming to think of the boy as flesh of his flesh.

And to think of Roni—not Marcy—as the boy's mother.

Which was craziness. Lunacy. He was *not* this boy's father. And Veronica Sykes was most certainly not the boy's mother any more than she was *his* wife.

Oh, yeah?

"How come I gotta go back to Nana then, Dad?" Pete raised his eyes at last and the plaintive accusation in them rendered Gerald temporarily mute.

Unable to speak, he stared with helpless frustration into the little boy's eyes. What could he say? How could he make it clear to the boy that this was nothing personal—

His thoughts careened to a halt here. *Whoa!* Nothing personal? You abandon the kid, you take him back to a person with whom he no longer belongs and you call that nothing personal?

So what have *you* been so damned sore about all these years, Moose m'boy? Remember, your mother's abandonment of you was nothing personal, either. And yet, all your life you've despised her for doing it....

Staring at Peter, hearing that inner voice, Gerald's chest got so tight he could hardly draw breath. He remembered how he'd felt as a kid, being passed from place to place, from home to home and, for reasons he'd either been too young or too ignorant to understand, always being found lacking in some way.

As Pete envisioned himself to be lacking?

"Damn it to hell—don't do this to me!" The words were an eruption of agony and frustration, a violent expression of opposition to forces outside of himself. Forces that seemed, once again, to be gaining the upper hand.

"No!" Dammit, he wouldn't allow it. Not this time.

"Peter," Gerald said hoarsely, drawing the frightened boy against his chest and tucking the small head beneath his chin. "Listen to me now. It's not that I don't want you. I... I love you, I really do. And I want... I want what's best for you. I do."

He stroked the fair head, pressed a kiss onto its crown. "I'm going to give your nana some money, and I'll send her more every month so that she can buy you all the stuff you need...."

As he held the boy and explained and cajoled, a part of Gerald grieved, while another part jeeringly wondered just who he was trying to convince here, himself or the kid?

But Gerald ruthlessly clamped down on every emotion and went on with his litany of justification and rationalization.

And less than an hour later, he and Pete were on their way again. To Barstow.

* * *

"It's been a while since we talked like this, pussycat," said Aunt Lou, somberly contemplating her niece across the expanse of quilt between them. "Not since before you got married, in fact." She paused and, when Roni continued to silently sit there and brood, she added, "I been watchin' you get sadder an' sadder ever since Pete and Gerald took off. You miss 'em, don't you?"

Roni's mouth tightened and its corners turned down. "I miss *him,*" she said in a voice constricted by tears she refused to shed. "Peter. That's all."

Louise let that go. "Gerald called twice today."

"I know. Leo told me."

"Why won't you talk to him?"

"There's nothing to say."

"Gerald seems to think there is, pussycat—"

"Gerald, Gerald," Roni flared, interrupting her aunt with a wild, burning glance. "That's all I've been hearing from you guys. He's all you care about."

"That's not true...."

"It *is* true," Roni contradicted heatedly. "None of you give a damn that he broke my heart when he took away—"

Her voice broke. She couldn't go on. Covering her eyes, she bit her lip and choked on a sob. "Damn," she said, dropping her hand and looking up at the ceiling to stem the ever-threatening tears. "I won't cry about this anymore. I won't...."

"Why not?" asked Louise with deliberate callousness. "Since you don't seem to have anything better to do these days."

She looked satisfied when Roni's affronted gaze clashed with hers, and added, "I've never seen such a case of 'poor me' in all my born days."

"Well . . . !" Face tight, Roni scrambled off the bed. "I can see I'm not going to get any sympathy here."

She marched to the door.

"Veronica." Louise's well-remembered listen-up-or-else tone made Roni stop with one hand on the doorknob. "Gerald said he'd be back here by tomorrow afternoon. . . ."

"Thanks for the warning." Roni refused to turn around. "I'll be sure to be out."

"He said he had a surprise for you."

"Well, I've got one for him, too," Roni said to the door. "Divorce papers."

When Louise didn't speak, Roni looked back across her shoulder. "That's what I came in here tonight to tell you, Aunt Lou. I went to see a lawyer this morning. He doesn't think the legalities will take long at all since there's no property involved and both of us are willing. . . ."

"What makes you think Gerald is willing, Veronica?"

Roni's eyes rounded. "You can ask that, knowing the way things have been between us ever since the wedding?"

Louise, scowling her displeasure with her niece, nodded. "Yeah, I can ask that." She paused; her gaze sharpened. "Seems to me, pussycat, that whatever it was that went wrong between the two of you, Gerald has done a lot of thinkin' and figurin' this past little while and that he's got somethin' to say to you. I think maybe you ought to stick around and listen, don't you?"

Trapped by her aunt's logic in spite of herself, Roni's heart began to beat like a kettledrum and it left her breathless. "Has...has he said anything to you...?"

Louise's determined expression softened along with her tone. "Only that you shouldn't do anything about anything until he'd had a chance to talk to you."

"When?" Roni could barely get the word out. What game was Gerald playing? she asked herself as she slowly made her way back to her aunt's bed and sank down at the edge of the mattress. And why did her justifiable anger at his perfidy no longer feel like anger but like excitement and—heaven help her—hope? "When did he say that, Aunt Lou?"

"Today. On the phone."

"And...and Peter? What did he say about Peter, Aunt Louise?"

At the pain in Roni's voice, and the tremulous hope, Louise's eyes clouded. She heaved a sigh. "Nothing, pussycat. I'm sorry, but he didn't mention little Petey at all...."

The private investigator's report couldn't begin to describe the dusty, dented and rusting wreck of a trailer to which the occupant of a similar abode a few miles up the road had directed them.

Sweet Mother Murphy. Was this the hovel where Pete had lived for most of his life? And was this where Marcy Kemp had hailed from, too?

Gerald was slow in turning off the engine, shocked by the squalor he beheld. The ramshackle trailer, listing to one side and with tattered rags in front of its grime-blinded windows, made the abandoned building in which he'd lived before prison seem like the Waldorf.

Pete, too, was looking wide-eyed and scared.

Gerald met his somber gaze with a shuttered one of his own. "This look familiar, Pete?" he asked.

Biting his lip, Pete nodded.

"Is this where your nana lives?"

"Uh-huh." The affirmation fell with difficulty from Peter's trembling lower lip.

Oh, man. Gerald closed his eyes against the misery in Pete's. It all came back to him now—how skinny Pete had been when he'd first come to Salem. How worn his clothes had been, and how dirty. How grubby, too, the little boy had been. Yet, he'd talked of his nana with love....

They were still sitting in the car, Pete frozen by apprehension and bewilderment, Gerald by an agony of indecision and rioting emotions, when the door of the trailer crashed open. An old man, filthy and disheveled, stood weaving in the opening, squinting against the brightness of day.

"Whaddaya wan'?" he hollered, clutching the doorjamb to keep himself upright.

"Joe," Pete said, going pale. "That's old Joe, Dad, and he's drunk."

"Git oudda here," the old man bellowed. "Git...!"

That sounded good to Gerald. Clearly, whether Pete's nana was still around or not, there was no way he would leave *his* boy in this kind of an environment. Face grim, he turned the key and started the engine.

But just then a small dog of indeterminable parentage came shooting out from behind the trailer, and, excitedly barking and yipping, came flying toward them across the trash-littered yard.

"Arf...!" In a flash, and before Gerald could in any way react, Pete was out of the car and on his knees with arms wide. The dog hurled itself into them and commenced licking and whimpering in an agony of joy that was mirrored in the ecstatic face Pete turned toward Gerald, who'd gotten out of the car.

"This is Arf, Dad," Pete said, tears streaming down his face. "He 'members me." He kissed the dog's head. "He loves me...."

Oh, God, and so do I, boy.

His throat clogged by emotion, and with the sting of tears burning the back of his eyelids, Gerald could only nod as he hunkered down beside Pete.

"You can pet him, if you want," Pete offered, with a smile so sweet it broke Gerald's heart. "I told Arf you're okay...."

"Thank you, son." *For the vote of confidence, and for the love I was almost to dumb not to treasure.*

Hesitantly, his hand no more steady than his voice had been, Gerald reached out to pat the dog's head. "They're gonna love him back at the boardinghouse," he said quietly after a while, and managed a shaky grin when Pete's eyes flew back to his and grew round.

"I'm sorry it took me so long to figure out that I need you much more than your nana ever could," he told Pete. "Sometimes even dads aren't very smart." He held out his hand. "Can you forgive me, son?"

His heart stopped, and the tears that had threatened rose up to blind him, when, in response to his words, Peter bent his head until it touched the dog's back, and bitterly wept.

With a choked curse, Gerald hauled boy and dog into his arms and pressed his own wet face close to Peter's. "I love you, Pete," he whispered hoarsely. "I love you so damned much. And I swear, I'll never hurt you or try to leave you again...."

The rest of their short stay outside of Barstow was an improvement over their initial welcome. Nana—Marie Kemp, now Ryerson because she and "Ol' Joe" were married—arrived on the scene moments later in a car that was in even worse condition than the trooper Gerald was driving, and just before her husband passed out cold on the doorstep.

The tenderness of her reunion with Peter went a long way toward disposing Gerald more kindly toward the woman. Whatever deprivations Pete had suffered while in her care, lack of love had not been one of them. Marie had done the best she could by the boy, and she said she appreciated Gerald's coming by with the boy to pick up the dog. Joe had wanted to get rid of him long ago, but Marie had hoped for just this day to come.

After refusing her offer of a meal, which Gerald was sure she could ill afford to share with him and Pete, he pressed all the money he could spare into her hand and, with promises to keep in touch, he, Peter and Arf took their leave.

Gerald tried repeatedly to get ahold of Roni to tell her that—finally—he'd come to his senses and seen the light. He was able to love, after all. He loved Peter. But, more than that and most important of all was that he was one hundred percent sure now that he loved Roni. He wanted her. Wanted her in his life, in the home he hoped to share with her and Pete, and in his bed.

For as long as it lasted . . . only this time he meant for it to last a lifetime. Forever.

Forever no longer sounded like prison doors clanging shut behind him, but rather like the gates of heaven opening to let him into paradise.

Beyond the barest necessities, Roni hadn't spoken to him since that final confrontation in the workshop. Not that he could blame her. He had taken all his frustrations and rioting emotions out on her, and the remark about being stuck with a wife he didn't want had been inexcusable.

And not true. If it ever had been, it certainly no longer was. He loved her, and even then he'd known it. But knowing and admitting it—even to himself—had been two different ball games. To him, and for too long, *love* had been a four-letter word he'd been as loath to utter as other people shunned those rude Anglo-Saxon ones he'd never batted an eye at. Love equated to pain in his life's reckoning.

Nothing had changed there, had it? he thought wryly as he stowed his duffel in the trunk and strapped Pete into his seat belt for the final leg home. Thinking of Roni, loving her and knowing she despised him, was giving him so much pain he wanted to cry out in agony.

And loving Pete, seeing the boy's trusting eyes and the love that shone from them . . . It hurt like hell to wonder if he was really deserving. And even more to know that he was not.

What could he offer this boy and this woman whom he loved? he asked himself desolately. A future with an ex-con whose past would probably come to haunt them again and again. For instance, not everybody at Mirashki Architects and Design had taken kindly to his past, which—not wanting any unwelcome surprises later—he'd made sure they all knew about. There'd been some whispers, some stares, some visible withdrawals; there always would be stuff like that going on. And it wouldn't always be aimed just at him, but at his family, too.

But then he recalled how fiercely Veronica had lit into the construction lead hand who'd been foolish enough to make a crack in her presence about Gerald's record. It had been about a week before the wedding, just before the strike. She'd come to the site to bring him his lunch, which had prompted the lead hand to remark on how unfair it was that criminals should have it so good, or words to that effect. Gerald would've just let the crack go, but not Veronica. Eyes spitting green flames, she'd cleaned the guy's clock with just a few well-chosen words that left him the butt of everybody else's needling for the rest of the day.

Remembering the guy's red-faced chagrin, Gerald chuckled. She was a fighter, his Roni, and if he could get her to stay with him, to give him a chance and to love him . . . why, then the future would surely take care of itself.

Rufus was barking.

Darn dog. Roni spared the neighbor's yard a jaundiced glance. And blast that Marge for always sticking the silly mutt outside whenever the urge to go someplace hit her and leaving others to listen to his yowling when all they wanted was a little peace and quiet.

Grimly Roni looked down at her weeding, wondering, was it her frazzled nerves or did Rufe sound more high-pitched and feverish than usual today?

Not likely the former—the dog weighed at least a hundred pounds and was a twelve-year-old male with an all-bass voice box. Moodily Roni yanked at some stubborn blackberry shoot and pricked her finger on a thorn. She rocked back on her heels with a cry of dismay that was way stronger than the negligible injury merited.

Damn. What was the matter with her? Tears pricked her eyelids as she popped the injured, dirt-encrusted finger into her mouth. It tasted of blood and earth. Yuk.

Totally at odds with herself and her environment, Roni covered her face with her hands and took a deep breath of earthy air. This has to stop, she told herself, peripherally aware that the barking noises seemed to be coming closer. She was losing her mind, and Gerald Marsden wasn't even worth it.

Where was he, anyway? If what Louise said was true, then he should've been here by now, shouldn't he?

And where was Peter? Had Gerald left him in Barstow? Would she really never see him again? Hold him again?

Peter.

Roni's shoulders slumped as her heartache intensified. How she missed that little guy. Even now, crouching here alone and miserable in the backyard of her boardinghouse, she thought she could hear his voice calling to her over that demented dog's high-pitched yip. She really *was* losing her mind. . . .

"Roni . . . ?" Pete was calling in that childish soprano his voice turned into when he got excited. "Roni, I'm home . . . !"

I'm home.

Roni dropped her hands. Her head snapped up and around toward the house. That voice was real. He was here.

"Petey . . . ?" A sound escaped her, half laugh, half sob.

He was really here. And staggering down the back steps with his arms full of a yapping, wriggling canine that he dropped the moment he caught sight of her there by the flower bed.

"Roni!" Arms windmilling, legs pumping, Pete flew across the lawn toward her as Rufus's woofs began to harmonize with the yips of the smaller dog at Pete's heels.

"Petey." Arms wide, Roni caught him in a fierce embrace as he hurled himself into them. The impact of his sturdy little body on hers toppled her, laughing and crying, backward into the grass and, for several heart-beats she and Pete lay there, gasping and incoherently babbling.

All too soon to suit Roni's need to hold on to the child, however, Pete was struggling out of her embrace. Talking a mile a minute, he introduced her to Arf, whose wildly wagging tail shook his entire body. Petting the cute little mongrel's scruffy black head, Roni discreetly wiped at the tears that kept welling up from some inner spring of emotion that would no longer be stopped. Peter was back.

And Gerald . . . ?

"Dad!"

Momentarily abandoned in favor of the tall, wide-shouldered man in T-shirt and blue jeans who stood on the back steps, Roni slowly got to her feet. Little by little, she raised streaming eyes until they blurrily connected with Gerald's deep blue ones. Motionless, she watched as he bent down to Peter, talked to the boy for a moment and then, with a pat on the rump, sent boy and dog scampering into the house.

"Cookies," he said, the faintly rough timbre of his baritone voice more pleasing to Roni's ears than the sweetest sonata. His pace leisurely—or was it hesi-tant?—he sauntered toward her. His gaze, intent, and alight with emotions Roni was afraid to guess at or analyze, was fixed on hers. "They're a pretty powerful bribe when they're homemade and shared by a kid's best friend."

About a foot away from Roni, Gerald stopped. "Or so I was told once," he added, "by this very smart teacher lady I know."

Roni's heart, which until that moment seemed to have stopped, began beating again. She remembered when she'd told Gerald that. It'd been one of the times she'd worked at bringing Gerald and Pete closer, and she'd sent Gerald up to the attic with a plate of homemade cookies.

"*That* day we were bribing him to make friends with you," she said, her still-moist eyes furtively, longingly scanning Gerald's face and noting with a pang how tired he looked. "What are you bribing him for this time?"

"Time to let me make friends with you," Gerald said huskily, reaching out and with one finger gently catching the tear that rolled down her cheek. "If you still want for us to be friends, that is."

All she'd ever wanted was for them to be friends. And more. Losing him had been hell, and not just because of Pete. If he was willing to stay now . . .

"I do," Roni said as a fresh supply of tears ran in rivers down her face. "For as long as it lasts. . . ."

"No." With his thumbs, Gerald stemmed the tears and caressed her quivering lips with a feather-light touch. "This time I'd want forever."

Forever. Roni's eyelids fluttered. "I'd like that."

"I've been such a damn fool, Veronica."

"No . . ." Her lids drifted shut completely and with a tremulous sigh, Roni leaned into the palm Gerald smoothed against the side of her face. When he didn't

move, when his fingers tensed along her jaw and still he
didn't speak, she opened her eyes again and was
shocked by the rawness she glimpsed in his.

"Gerald . . . ?"

He swallowed, but his eyes on hers were unwavering
and, in spite of the anguish there, they were true. "I
love you, Veronica," he said, and his voice trembled
with the intensity of what he felt and needed to convey.
"I love you."

"Oh, Gerald . . ." Her own love vibrating through that
soft exhalation of his name, Roni took the short step to
close the space that still separated their bodies.

And then she was in his arms, with her own wrapped
around his neck. Urgently, needily, their lips met,
joined, searched and tasted. And, as always, passion
flared instantly like a bonfire between them, only this
time there was love to both temper and fan the flames
into something so hot, it forged them together forever.

And on the back steps, watching the fiery reunion,
stood little Pete with Arf in his arms and his mouth
hanging open. Behind him Aunt Lou and old Miz
Henks dabbed at their eyes, while the judge forcefully
harrumphed and Leo trumpeted into his handkerchief.

"Oh, for Pete's sake," the judge said, looking as
proud and pleased as if he'd arranged this happy ending single-handedly himself. "Will you look at them
lovebirds. . . ."

*   *   *   *   *

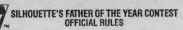

SILHOUETTE'S FATHER OF THE YEAR CONTEST
OFFICIAL RULES

Here's how to enter:

1. On one side of an 8½" × 11" piece of paper to which you have attached a photograph of your father, hand print or type your name, address, the name of your father, and in 200 words or fewer, tell us why your father is so fabulous.

2. Mail your completed entry (limit one per envelope) via first-class mail to: SILHOUETTE'S FATHER OF THE YEAR CONTEST, 3010 Walden Avenue, P.O. Box 9046, Buffalo, NY 14269-9046 if mailing from U.S., or SILHOUETTE'S FATHER OF THE YEAR CONTEST, P.O. Box 613, Fort Erie, Ontario L2A 5X3, if mailing from Canada. All entries must be received no later than 9/30/93. No responsibility is assumed for lost, late or misdirected mail.

3. Entries will be judged on the basis of sensitivity—60%—and appropriateness—40%—of the essay. All entries and photographs become the property of Harlequin Enterprises, Ltd. and may be used for advertising, merchandising or publicity purposes. No correspondence will be answered. Only one prize will be awarded. The winner will be selected no later than 10/31/93 and notified by mail. Prize consists of a Fab Dad Sweatshirt and Book Collection (value: $75 U.S.).

4. Contest open to residents of U.S. and Canada. Employees of Torstar Corporation, D.L. Blair, Inc., their affiliates, subsidiaries, advertising, printing and promotional agencies and members of their immediate families are not eligible. Tax liability on prize is the sole responsibility of winner. Contest is void wherever prohibited and is subject to all Federal, State and local laws and regulations.

5. Potential winner must execute and return an Affidavit of Eligibility and Publicity Release within 30 days of notification or an alternate winner may be selected. Entry and acceptance of prize offered constitutes permission to use winner's/father's name and/or likeness, for purposes of advertising and trade on behalf of Harlequin Enterprises, Ltd., without further compensation unless prohibited by law.

6. For the name of the winner (available after 11/30/93), send a self-addressed, stamped envelope to: Silhouette's Father of the Year Contest Winner, P.O. Box 4200, Blair, NE 68009.

SRFDRUL

Take 4 bestselling love stories FREE

Plus get a FREE surprise gift!

Now you can enter your

in Silhouette Romance's
"FATHER OF THE YEAR" contest
and win great prizes for both of you!

Simply write to Silhouette, telling us why your father is so fabulous, and include a photo of him. Entry coupons and details can be found inside any of the June, July or August FABULOUS FATHER titles. The winning father will have his photo placed in the inside back cover of the June 1994 Fabulous Father title and the winning letter will be placed in the back pages of the same title. In addition, the FATHER OF THE YEAR will receive a great FABULOUS FATHER sweatshirt and the submitter will receive a complete set of 1993 FAB DAD books to enjoy.

To enter the Silhouette Romance FATHER OF THE YEAR Contest, fill out the coupon below with *your* name, address, and zip or postal code and enclose it with your letter and photo to:

In the U.S.	**In Canada**
Silhouette Romance	Silhouette Romance
FATHER OF THE YEAR Contest	FATHER OF THE YEAR Contest
3010 Walden Avenue	P.O. Box 613
P.O. Box 9046	Fort Erie, Ontario
Buffalo, NY 14269-9046	L2A 5X3

Your Name: _____
Address: _____
City: _____ State/Prov.: _____
Zip/Postal: _____
Your Father's Name: _____
Place where you purchased your Fabulous Father title: _____

KAZ

(Contest entry deadline is September 30, 1993. See previous page for
full contest details.)

SRFDPOP